The
Three Widows
of Wylder

by

Julie Howard

The Wylder West

The Three Widows of Wylder

COPYRIGHT © 2021 by Julie Howard

Cover Art by *The Wild Rose Press, Inc.*

The Wild Rose Press, Inc.
PO Box 708
Adams Basin, NY 14410-0708
Visit us at www.thewildrosepress.com

Publishing History
First Edition, 2021
Trade Paperback ISBN 978-1-5092-3905-4
Digital ISBN 978-1-5092-3906-1

The Wylder West
Published in the United States of America

Emma stood, legs apart, one hand on the pistol at her hip. The covered wagon was old, the type used years ago by pioneers, before trains tamed the prairie, and they still lumbered across areas where tracks hadn't been laid. Two women sat side-by-side, too focused on their argument to yet notice the camp they entered. Their one horse, overmatched by the heavy wagon, was damp with sweat, its mouth flecked with froth.

"We should have stayed on the main road." The peevish one appeared much younger, curly gold hair topped by a large straw hat. She wore a light-yellow dress with lace at her wrists and throat, a perfectly inadequate outfit for travel. "Someone could have provided directions."

The older woman had finely-drawn features; a few strands of gray threaded through uncovered dark hair. Dressed in sensible blue calico, she gripped the reins too tight and the poor horse gave a pathetic shake of its head. "The whole point was to avoid people."

Emma strode forward and seized the reins. "For God's sake, you're killing him."

The two women gaped as though they were staring at an apparition. The horse, released from harsh hands, lowered its head and halted. Its sides heaved as flies drank at its sweaty flanks.

"Whoever let you fools handle a horse should be whipped." Emma dropped one hand back to her pistol, tempted to dispatch the women to hell for their cruelty.

Praise for Julie Howard

THE THREE WIDOWS OF WYLDER:
"A captivating read…a wonderfully imagined tale of three women each with her own dark secret who are on the run to escape their pasts. An engaging story of hope and redemption."

~Mirella Sichirollo Patzer, author
~*~

"Absolute praise for a hilarious yet touching race west for three women with nothing in common but the murders they want to leave behind. Utterly enjoyable!"

~Colleen L. Donnelly, author of Out of Splinters and Ashes *and* Mine to Tell
~*~

HOUSE OF SEVEN SPIRITS:
"What a great mystery! Ms. Howard combines suspense, romance, vengeance and ghosts to weave a story that's engrossing from page one."

~InD'Tale Magazine Crowned Heart review
~*~

SPIRIT IN TIME:
"Julie Howard's writing is sublime."

~NN Light Book Heaven

Dedication

To all the tough, unheralded women throughout history
who persevered despite the odds

Chapter One
Clara

Divorce.

Clara Walker slapped the faded red and gray checked shirt into the soapy wash basin with a splash. She scrubbed her husband's shirt against the rippled washboard with months of pent-up fury. A line of flapping laundry snapped in a gust of wind across the yard as if to punctuate her musings. Why so much fuss about divorce when it was clear she and Walter weren't suited for each other? They married too young. She'd been foolish, and he'd been rash.

The cool water eased the ache in her hands. Nineteen years ago, she had the reputation as the prettiest gal in Platte County, maybe in all of Missouri. Walter latched onto her quicker than mud on a hog. He sweet-talked his hand into her bodice, then under her skirt. Minnie Turner confided to her after church one Sunday that was how a girl got babies. So when he asked her to marry him, she said yes in a hurry. Pappy would kill her if her stomach swelled up big and round.

Only, fingers didn't get you pregnant. She learned that unpleasant fact two hours after the preacher declared them man and wife. Men had another finger below their belly button that swelled up big as a turnip each night. Minnie apparently didn't know about that extra appendage. Walter had been twenty-two and she was a month shy of her seventeenth birthday. And wouldn't you know? Nineteen years of putting that extra finger to use and Walter still hadn't given her a baby.

Divorce.

The way her husband reacted, you'd think Clara asked for a house lit by electricity like they started doing in New York City. Didn't the Bible say something about being unevenly yoked? Or about marrying in haste? Maybe the latter wasn't from the Bible, but somebody smart said it. Probably a woman. Because who repented for marriage more than a woman?

A gopher popped his russet-brown head up from its hole near the laundry line. The bold little fellow and his family would dig through her garden, chew her petunias and nibble the tender broccoli shoots. But she hadn't the heart to go after him. His whiskered nose twitched once before he ducked out of sight.

Damnation. A hole appeared in a side seam of the shirt. She sat back on her heels. This was Walter's favorite shirt and she would have to sew it that evening. If they had children, she'd make miniature clothes for dolls and toy soldiers. She would enjoy baking biscuits and pies to elicit smiles on their bright faces. Life would finally have meaning. She might sing little ones to sleep at night and breathe in their sweet scents. Instead, each night, she lay abed with a turnip.

Walter's voice boomed out the window. "Clara! I need you."

The shirt slipped from her hands into the sudsy water. She untied her washing apron and laid it on a chair to dry before going inside the house. Their home doubled as Walter's medical practice and apothecary. He examined patients in a front room, and dispensed medical cures from a large glass-fronted cabinet kept in their kitchen. Each drawer in the bottom third of the heavy walnut cabinet stored dried herbs and flowers she harvested at their peak season. Above, behind the glass, were vials and boxes that contained the "real" medicine Walter obtained from a colleague in Kansas City. This was the perfect analogy for their marriage—his life on view and in the dominant position, hers dried up and hidden away.

He met her in the kitchen, his voice low. "Mrs. Wilson has a female complaint. I told her you will speak to her. Nothing pains her but what is inside her head. Give her one of your tea blends."

She gave a short nod and headed to their small parlor—the room deemed appropriate for her sessions with female patients. If Walter believed a woman hysterical, with her troubles emanating from a frail mind, he'd call in Clara to offer one of her tinctures or herbal teas. Calm the woman, make her placid and agreeable, and send her on her way. That was her job. Walter considered his time too important to waste on trivialities.

The parlor's white lace curtains filtered the afternoon sun. The patient, in her late fifties with gray hair covered under a straw hat topped with a blue feather, was squeezed into a dress at least one size too small for her generous middle. Any fool could see looser attire might alleviate the woman's short breath, anxiety and fainting spells.

Clara shut the door behind her. "Mrs. Wilson, what a lovely blue shawl and matching feather."

The woman gave a pleased smile. "Thank you, Clara. It's good to see you well. We all missed you at church the past few Sundays."

"Yes, I—"

"Dr. Walker sat in the pew by himself. We all remarked how lonely he looked, no wife by his side. I expect we'll see you this Sunday, since you appear quite recovered from whatever ailed you."

"I might—"

"Dr. Walker is the dearest man. You are a very lucky girl. He was quite the catch for a farm girl such as yourself."

Annoyed at the woman's overbearing manner, Clara spoke quickly. "Yes, Mrs. Wilson, I know. You remind me of this every time I see you. For nearly twenty years now."

"An *educated* man. And handsome. The Hill sisters were quite devastated when the banns went up for your marriage. Of course, they're both married now, with several children each." The woman frowned at this last bit, clearly a chastisement to Clara for not fulfilling her own wifely duty and supplying her husband with a brood of his own.

The words stung. Tears threatened, and she gritted her teeth. She refused to cry in front of the old busybody. "I suppose they made the better choice, with husbands able to give them children."

The older woman gasped. "It's a spiteful girl who places that burden on her husband."

In for a penny, in for a pound, as Clara's mother always said. "You *are* aware of how babies are made, aren't you? Dr. Walker is equally involved."

"Indecent. I didn't come here to listen to your

private business." The woman rose with a huff. "Does your husband know you speak in this manner to his patients? He said you would give me a tincture for my pains, but anything you'd offer is likely to poison me."

Mrs. Wilson stalked out of the room and the front door slammed a moment later. Oh, why had she let her tongue run loose like that? The woman had pricked an open wound. Their childless state might not be Walter's fault. She could be barren. Wouldn't it be best for them to go their separate ways and try with someone else? Thirty-six might not be too old. Her arms ached to hold a child.

Divorce.

****

"Lord, Clara. You have but one job and you've failed at that."

A book lay open on the supper table next to his soup bowl. A pair of reading glasses perched halfway down his nose and his cool, light-blue eyes examined her over the lenses as though he delivered a terminal diagnosis in that annoying matter-of-fact tone. "Why did you have to go and offend Mrs. Wilson? All you needed to do was give her a packet of tea."

She stared into her barley soup, flaked with bits of beef left over from the previous night's dinner. A bit too much salt. The oregano awakened her taste buds though. It didn't serve to react to Walter's grievance. Time had taught her to hide emotions behind few words.

"She insulted me."

"If Mrs. Wilson switches to Dr. Millhouse, she'll take half the ladies in town with her. She wields a great deal of influence. I send you in to the women as part of our livelihood, not a social hour." Walter's usual critique of her day flowed seamlessly to another topic. "I noticed my shirt in your sewing basket."

"A seam opened up."

"As long as I can wear it in the morning."

She rose and served him a slice of fried chicken and mashed turnips, her own bitter joke. The bowls of food sat right in front of him, but he insisted on being served, just as his mother had done for his father. Thirty-six years old with decades of this dull, meaningless life ahead. She couldn't bear the thought. *I may die of despair.*

"Walter," she began, perched on her chair, without filling her plate.

"Don't start." He sipped his water, beer reserved for Saturday dinners. "The subject is closed."

"For both our sakes. Before we're too old."

Her husband took one, two, three bites of fried chicken and chewed each piece thoroughly before swallowing. Walter had a dread of choking, the way his father died a decade earlier. Only then did he respond, in his usual, even tone. "We will not divorce. Do you want to ruin the business I've built here? Mother warned me not to marry you, but I insisted. I made my bed and now will sleep in it." He flipped a page and lowered his head to the book.

"What nonsense, when there's a way out." Her voice rose despite her resolve to remain calm, and he frowned at his book. "Mrs. Elizabeth Cady Stanton says a woman should have the ability to divorce without her husband's permission. She says this right is every bit as important as the right to vote."

His fist crashed down on the table. "Do *not*

mention that ridiculous woman's name in my house." His voice shook in rage and a small part of her was glad to have roused some emotion in him. "And do *not* lecture me."

"Mrs. Stanton claims justly that the Bible, put together by men, makes women to be little more than slaves. I can't help if this makes me wonder about church and its teachings." She raced forward while she had his attention, even if his eyebrows were lowered and his glare dangerous. "Admit you don't love me. I'm happy to say I no longer love you."

A supercilious smile crept to his lips. "Love at our age. A childish notion by a childish mind. The Bible protects women who cannot reason like men." Walter dabbed a napkin to his mouth. "The soup was a little salty tonight."

After he closed the book with a snap and left the table, she slumped in her seat. The aroma of dinner now repellent. Children's laughter drifted through the open window on a breeze. Her heart clenched.

****

Minnie Turner, whose last name had been Sanders for the past sixteen years, never said in one word what could be said in ten. The moment Clara entered her modest wood frame house the next afternoon, her friend gushed forth with the latest gossip. "You remember Eliza Perkins, who lost her husband to infection last spring? She's running the farm by herself and says it's never performed better. Corn and wheat came in fine last summer—and she bought the Murphy place adjacent. You know the one with the big front porch and pretty picture window. Plans to turn the farmhouse over to the manager."

7

They settled in for a proper chat in Minnie's messy kitchen, an egg-crusted pan still on the stove, the wood crate empty, mismatched dishes stacked haphazardly on a shelf. Oat cookies lay on a blue ironstone china platter in the middle of a rough-hewn table where they sat. The Sanders didn't have a proper parlor, a room only rich folk had as they were the only ones with the time to sit around and do nothing.

Minnie exempted Clara and Walter from this disparagement since they used their parlor for business. In her late thirties, sinews stretched taut in Minnie's neck and blue veins bulged on the back of her hands like a much older woman. Her friend had married a man who drank most of what he earned, and she took in laundry and sewing to keep their four children fed. Clara understood Minnie secretly wished for a little idle time and a parlor to spend it in.

"I received a letter from Marcus yesterday."

Clara slid the envelope from her dress pocket. Her brother, the only family she had left in the world, wrote once or twice a year from his farm in the Wyoming Territory. She treasured his letters filled with descriptions of "freedom a man can chew on and emerald mountains that rise to the sky." "He says a woman there became justice of the peace."

Minnie's eyes widened as she poured out two glasses of lemonade. "Women vote there, don't they? I can't imagine. Do they wear pants and crop their hair short like men?"

Clara laughed at her friend's simple understanding. "They wear exactly what they wore before they got the vote."

"I wouldn't know what to vote for," Minnie said.

"Who has the time, with so much to do at home? Thomas doesn't read and I've gotten out of the habit, except for the Bible."

Clara fingered the letter, the thick paper crackling in her hands. She had hoped to read the letter out loud, so she might enjoy her brother's words all over again. "Marcus doesn't approve of women's suffrage, but he's a good man."

"Eliza Perkins' husband was a good man. Left her comfortable. A widow can own property, with all the rights of a man. Isn't that a fine thing? If Thomas died, I suppose the railroad might employ my oldest. Fourteen's old enough." All innocence, Minnie blinked. "And how is Walter and his stomach complaint these days?"

"Healthier than our mule," she grumbled before she realized how terrible this must sound to her friend. "I mean to say perhaps he overstates his pain from time to time. He'll see me buried before he's in the grave." She stopped. Her mouth often flapped before her brain caught up. Why talk about Walter and death to her gossipy friend?

Minnie's dark eyes danced with mischief. Her childhood friend understood her too well. "You don't know when the good Lord might lay claim on him. Might be any day. You could be a widow before the year's out and, my goodness, you'd be a woman with property. You got lucky with Walter."

Clara's hand, outstretched for a second cookie, paused in mid-air. Widowhood. If Walter died, not only would she be free, but the house and four hundred dollars in savings would be hers. If she remarried in a year, the possibility of a child still existed. Her life

9

might be on the cusp of renewal. Any day, any moment.

"You must have a poison or two in that kitchen of yours," Minnie continued, her tone light and teasing. "Poof. Goodbye husband."

The leaves of rhubarb, foxglove, jack-in-the-pulpit, belladonna. Her mother taught her everything she knew about healing plants and herbs; what to avoid and therefore what killed. Her breath came quicker. She chewed the oat cookie, which now tasted like sawdust in her mouth.

The conversation meandered to summer gardens, the latest Montgomery Ward catalog, the brash behavior of other people's children, and the recent shooting death of the outlaw Jesse James on the other side of Platte City.

Through it all, Clara couldn't stop thinking about the widow Eliza Perkins.

****

Walter laid down his cloth napkin next to his plate several days after her visit with Minnie. As his first patient of the day was expected soon, he devoured his usual two poached eggs, ham steak and biscuits heaped with butter within minutes. "Reverend Miller will stop by to visit this afternoon."

Clara's heart sank. Likely the good Methodist reverend was on a mission to round up his stray lamb and return her to the fold. "Yes, of course."

His cool gaze appraised her face and when there was no further response, he grunted and headed to his office. She cleared the table, washed the dishes and pans, and inventoried the pantry for items she needed at the mercantile the next day. Why, oh why had Minnie put the idea of Walter's death in her head? Now it muddled her thoughts. Perhaps Rev. Miller's duty call would soothe her unfulfilled heart.

Birdsong rose through the kitchen window. The chirps and trills of the cardinal, merry song of the robin, prayerful call of the titmouse. They blended into a spirited orchestra. The warm spring morning promised a glorious day ahead, a welcome relief from the past harsh winter. She planned to traipse through the woods and collect new growth of rose hips to ease Walter's stomach pains, wild ginger for "female complaints," and the bark of the Tree-of-Heaven for fever.

The front door opened and closed. The murmur of deep voices told her Walter's patients had arrived. This was a light day in her husband's schedule, and he planned to catch up on medical journals in the afternoon. Her trivial services were not required today and so she could fashion her own agenda.

The stroll through the woods behind their house did more for her spiritual state than church ever did. God spoke to her through the soft brush of ferns, rustle of green leaves in the breeze, and scent of wild apple trees in their annual pink profusion of bloom. Along with healing plants, she gathered a cluster of violets to display for the reverend's visit. As with all things in nature, God had a plan for her. If the Creator meant for her to be childless, then she needed to accept it. So unfair, when Minnie had four children she could barely afford to keep!

By the time she returned to the house, all was quiet. She tapped on Walter's office door to offer lunch, but when he didn't respond, she slipped back to the kitchen with his sandwich. He didn't like to be disturbed when he was deep in study.

Minnie's voice traveled through the window and Clara glanced out to observe her friend coming up the walk with the reverend. On their heels was an iron-faced Mrs. Wilson. Goodness. She needed to set out two more teacups and plates for cake.

"Good afternoon, Reverend. Mrs. Wilson." She gave the older woman a nod who responded with a frown. "Hello, Minnie."

"I ran into the reverend and Mrs. Wilson on the street, and who were they on their way to see but my good friend Clara," Minnie said. "'The more the merrier,' I always say."

"Of course. You are always welcome." Her friend knew she'd serve cake and tea to the reverend. "We can sit in the parlor."

Rev. Miller stroked his heavy mustache and didn't budge from his spot in the entryway. "Where is the good doctor? I thought he could join us."

Clara gave a nervous laugh. "He's been in his office all day. I doubt he will want to be disturbed. Let me get some refreshments. I made a raisin cake."

"Never mind the cake," Mrs. Wilson said briskly. "Fetch your husband, Clara. He should be here while the reverend speaks. Your soul is of the utmost importance."

Clara hesitated, but the reverend nodded in agreement. Walter must hear every word through his office door, but he didn't emerge. He would blame her for this interruption. "I can tell him all about our conversation later."

Mrs. Wilson brushed past her and rapped on the office door. "Dr. Walker, we'd like your attendance."

Nervous at bothering Walter, Clara touched her on

the shoulder. "Mrs. Wilson, please."

The woman rapped again, louder this time. "Why doesn't he answer?"

The reverend joined them at the door, the three of them with shoulders touching. Minnie stood on her tiptoes behind them, her breath on Clara's neck.

"Perhaps he's gone out," the reverend suggested.

"Nonsense," Mrs. Wilson said. "He was aware of our vital mission today." In one quick motion, she twisted the knob and thrust open the door. "Dr. Walker, pardon the intrusion—"

Her mouth gaped.

Clara stepped inside. "Walter?"

Her husband lay flat on his back, one leg bent and crooked to the side, hands with palms up like a final supplication. A fly crawled across one palm. An indelicate amount of light blared through the window for the tableau it illuminated. One window was open and a breeze had carried a few papers to the floor. The scene was so unlike her husband that she comprehended at once he must be dead.

She crossed the room quickly. "Walter."

She fell to her knees next to him. How long had he lain here? While she wandered in the woods? Made his sandwich?

"Oh, my heaven and earth, the doctor is gone." Mrs. Wilson's shocked voice reminded her the others gathered in the room. "What could have happened to him?" Her eyes narrowed as they settled on Clara.

The reverend's lips moved under his thick mustache as he muttered a prayer. He too stared at her. A prickle of fear traveled up her neck.

Minnie's mouth gaped open. For the first time,

Clara noted how much like a fish her best friend looked. If anyone had the ability to help her now, it was Minnie. But her best friend's words spoke otherwise.

"Oh Clara! What have you done?"

Chapter Two
Mary Rose

Third time's a charm.

Mary Rose Culver hummed a tune as she fingered the new selection of ribbons in the only general store for Emporia, Kansas. Pink or lavender? She sighed. She wasn't a young girl anymore who could claim a blushing pink, but the dull colors of a matron weren't right either. Something fresh, a bright hue to draw an appreciative eye or envious regard.

At fifty-two, Josiah Culver was much too old for her. Nearly a thirty-year difference. But a mature man had means, a lifetime of accumulated wealth and—to be frank—not many years ahead. Mary Rose intended to put in her time and be a rich widow within the decade. Not like her first husband, Patrick, who struggled to pay the rent. But, my oh my, he had made her knees go weak with just a glance.

Her mother, of a formidable nature and who dispensed advice in lieu of nurturing arms, warned her not to waste her youth and pretty blonde curls on a local farmhand. Marry young and often, her mother coached. That's how women get ahead in the world.

Marry the first time for reputation, the second for wealth, the third for love.

Mary Rose tripped up the first time. Patrick O'Connell's green eyes and silky way with words got

her to the altar at sixteen. Oh, that first year was a
marvel of adoration and nighttime sensations. Then she
lost one child to miscarriage, and then another. Her
mother didn't need to say a thing; Mary Rose knew she
had disturbed the world's perfect order of things. Or
rather, her mother's perfect order of things. Patrick had
to go.

"Shall I wrap up some of those ribbons for you,
Mrs. Culver?" The store owner rocked onto his toes and
back on his heels, up and down like a seesaw. The
man's rusty sideburns sprang forth as though a horse's
mane clung to either side of his face.

She smiled, a purse of her lips that showed off the
dimple in her cheek, knowing how it affected men.
Silly creatures. So easy to manipulate. "I'm afraid Mr.
Culver has curtailed my allowance for ribbons. He
believes three or four are plenty." She laughed. "He
hasn't much experience with women, I'm afraid."

The store owner crept closer. She lowered her eyes,
aware of the pretty picture her dark eyelashes made
against her pale skin and waited.

"I don't suppose one little ribbon would hurt. A
little gift from me." The man's breath reeked of onions
as well as the whiskey he kept behind the counter. "I
understand women," he cleared his throat, "and their
needs. It will be our secret."

She giggled and edged out of hand's reach, careful
not to overplay her role. Her goal was to inspire
respectful admiration, not a man's base hankerings.
"You are very kind."

The door to the mercantile banged open and two
men entered. The owner's mouth twisted. "Pick out
what you'd like," he said in a more abrupt tone, and

hurried to his other customers.

With a tangerine-colored ribbon nestled in her pocketbook next to her allowance, she waved goodbye a moment later. Josiah didn't give a hoot if she spent the money on frippery; he insisted she dress well as her appearance added to his prestige. She enjoyed the challenge and practice of molding men to her will. Beauty was fleeting, her mother tutored, but a skilled woman could charm the opposite sex for decades past her youthful prime.

A stiff breeze ruffled her curls and a dust devil kicked up in the street. The whirlwind caught up a broadsheet from the bench in front of the barbershop, and then appropriated a straw hat from Mr. Evans, second-in-charge at the savings and loan. The man chased his hat into the street and collided with one of those new-fangled high-wheel bicycles, knocking the rider from his tall perch. The two fellows started arguing while the hat tumbled end over end until it was crushed under the mail carriage, just in from Colorado. The dust devil waned into a low eddy as Mary Rose lifted her skirts and crossed to where the coach had stopped.

The coachman tipped his broad hat in greeting. She often met the coach, known as a "mud wagon," so named because its tall wheels rolled easily through muddy roads. Instead of the usual weekly missive, the last time her mother wrote was almost two months ago. Surely, there would be a letter by now. Mary Rose had written several times, each more urgent in tone than the last. Why didn't her mother reply?

Passengers tumbled out of the coach, their faces drawn with exhaustion from the crowded and dusty journey. Although the Atchison, Topeka and Santa Fe Railway covered the same distance in a fraction of the time, the mail coach was less expensive. Sweat flecked the four horses and their nostrils flared from a hard day's work. They seemed to know this was their destination, with oats and a rubdown waiting, and shook the harness with impatience.

There was no point in hovering. The mail had to be delivered to the post office for distribution. That was the law. But Mary Rose couldn't help herself. Something was wrong with her mother. Josiah shrugged off the delay. His own family was back East, two brothers and an elderly aunt who didn't communicate from one year to the next.

She suspected he didn't mind her mother far removed. "A married woman shall be guided by her husband," he had declared.

Turned out, Josiah was bossier than she anticipated, grown far too confident after their wedding, only five months earlier. Well, wealthy men required conceit to rise in status. He was fifty-two, she reminded herself again, with gray hairs sprouting from all manner of unnatural places, and in the final phase of his life.

The coachman and his two-man crew tossed down passengers' luggage from the rack on the rooftop. Mary Rose continued on her way to the Episcopalian church, where she had taken her wedding vows. Her dress a beautiful creation, white though this wasn't her first marriage, high-necked with lace at her wrists, and with a veil for Josiah to lift and kiss his bride. Satin slippers had caressed her feet. She had been a vision to behold, so everyone said.

Her new husband presented her with a modest

diamond ring at the altar, smaller than she believed fitting for her place in society. Josiah liked to be well-thought of, with public donations to the widow's fund and boastful declarations about his possessions, but he also kept one eye on the bottom line.

Inside the empty church, a huge cross hung above the altar. She arranged her skirts around her in the front pew and lowered her head. *Please, let there be a letter today. Take care of my two lost babies in Heaven. Forgive my mother her sins.* She wracked her brain for any other prayers she might offer, but none surfaced. She sat a bit longer so God, or anyone else who might be about, wouldn't think less of her for being in a hurry.

When a decent amount of time passed, she hastened to the post office, where several people queued at the counter.

"Nothing today, Mrs. Culver." The postman, a pale man who appeared as though he spent all his time indoors, pursed his lips when she reached the front of the line.

She didn't need a menial clerk to pity her and gossip. "No matter," she said in a bright voice. "I was walking past and thought I'd check if there is important news for my husband."

"Of course."

The man didn't appear convinced. All her letters to her mother passed through his hands. He knew she waited for a reply. She held her head high and swept out of the office. If she were braver, she'd ask him to send a telegram, but he would read her words: *Mother, please, please write. I need you. I'm worried for you.*

In all her twenty-five years, this was the longest she had gone without her mother's advice. She hadn't always heeded the counsel, but she listened and learned.

Mary Rose halted on the boardwalk. Her mouth dropped open before she caught herself and pressed her lips together. A idea occurred to her. This absence of communication, this silence, was nothing more than another lesson. *Learn to stand on your own two feet.* She almost laughed in relief. Wasn't this just like her mother, to also teach in subtle ways. With a spring in her step, she headed home.

****

"Dinner should be served at six in future, please." Josiah's frowning countenance appeared at the kitchen door. "My constitution needs plenty of time for digestion before bedtime."

"Yes, dear." Mary Rose gave him her dimpled smile, even though annoyance rippled through her. "If I rehired your previous cook, dinner would never be late."

He chuckled, his grimace replaced by amusement. "My sweet little wife, so young and imprudent. There's only two of us in the house and you have nothing to do but take care of me. Perhaps when our children come, we can hire some help."

The beefsteak sizzled in the cast iron skillet and she scraped at the blackened surface. This damned new charcoal stove cooked hotter than the wood ones she was accustomed to. Josiah was willing to spend money on a fancy, new stove, but not on household help.

Imprudent. Thomas had used that word about her, too. Her second husband had been a bank accountant, solid enough in reputation to satisfy her mother. At twenty and freshly widowed—poor Patrick having taken ill that spring—she was still pert and lively enough to entice any man in her hometown of Colorado Springs. Patrick's death left her with nothing but his farming tools and rent due on their small cabin.

Back in her mother's house, they plotted her next endeavor. Thomas Fisher was twenty-eight, with clean nails, and wore a suit to work. He strode through the streets promptly at seven-thirty each morning, and back again at six p.m. Coincidentally, Mary Rose strolled along the same path each evening. One quick smile, then a hello. He tipped his hat and by the second week, he knew her name. Three months later, they were engaged.

For the first time in her life, Mary Rose didn't have to buy groceries on credit. Thomas gave her a household allowance. She squirreled away a percentage each week, remembering how she'd been left broke after her first husband's demise. Thomas uncovered the stash in her delicates' drawer, one Sunday.

"Why were you pawing through my private things?" she demanded, hands on hips.

He ignored her question and asked a series of his own: "Where did this money come from and why is it hidden from me? What else are you hiding?"

From that moment on, he audited all she spent. He came home at odd hours of the day to check on her. A year into their marriage, he struck her for the first time. She was "imprudent" in her ways.

She cried her woes into her mother's shoulder. Subsequently, Thomas grew steadily ill, with bouts of vomiting for two months before he died.

Few men were interested in courting a woman widowed twice over at the age of twenty-two. Unbeknownst to Mary Rose, her mother placed an advertisement in four cities, including the Emporia newspaper. *Young beauty seeks kind, older man for respectable marriage. Cooks, cleans, complaisant nature.*

Twenty-two men wrote back, all over the age of forty-five, citing their advantages as though they applied for a job. Three well-heeled men rose to the top of the pile, and letters were exchanged. Josiah Culver was the only one who didn't ask questions about her previous marriage—they'd decided not to mention the union with Patrick. He also owned a two-story house along with a small carriage factory and had no children. After a respectable length of correspondence, Josiah sent a train ticket and declared he would marry her upon an "in-person inspection."

Imprudent. The word rankled. Hadn't she saved Josiah the cost of a ribbon that very afternoon by shrewd ingenuity? This, and other little faults, had crowded her letters to her mother. *Josiah may not be the right man for me after all*, she had written.

She stabbed the beefsteak with a fork and dark pink juices flooded out. Cooked enough. A clever girl like her should be able to handle a staid, practically prehistoric husband. But a decade's worth of her last bloom of youth with a man in his dotage!

He waited at the table, a glass of burgundy wine in one hand, bulbous nose flushed with its effect. She set down their plates of beef, mashed potatoes, and boiled carrots, and he dug in with gusto. Liver spots marred the backs of his hands; his pants unbuttoned at the top for comfort. She hadn't fully considered the sacrifice required, how boring life was with a man incurious about his neighbors' habits, no gossip to share at the end of the day, few social connections. Marriage by mail had coughed up this tedious drudge, the residue of the local matrimonial pool that no other female wanted.

Josiah belched and rubbed his substantial gut. "Delicious, dear. Very juicy meat. Why hire my old cook back when a much better one is right in front of my eyes? It was my lucky day when you arrived on that train. Yes indeed." He tucked his small chin down and gave her an adoring gaze, a speck of gravy at the side of his fleshy lips.

Her mother's words came to her then, as though her very spirit was in the room, proffering guidance. *Put what you've learned to use. Do this one yourself.*

****

The question was how. She didn't have access to arsenic, her mother's secret weapon. She must remain above suspicion, the model of a loving, dutiful wife. The key was to leave no trail, especially since her previous husbands died in similar ways. In case an unnatural death was ever suspected, she couldn't purchase rat poison. As the days dragged on, her decision to kill Josiah never wavered. Mother would be proud of her clear-sightedness and determination to handle things herself, which clearly was the intent of her mother's silence.

A week later, fate arrived breathless and disheveled at her door.

"Mary Rose!" Her husband's jovial voice bounced down the hallway to the little room she had claimed as her own, for sewing, reading and afternoon naps. "We have a visitor."

She started up from the settee's soft cushion, her heart suddenly racing. "Mother," she whispered, and raced for the front door. A pale, dark-haired woman with haunted brown eyes stared at her from behind Josiah's wide back. Two large satchels were in his hands.

"My wife, Mary Rose," her husband announced, "meet Edwina Perkins. Mrs. Perkins inquired about a horse cart and—" he chuckled, "—I had to inform her my carriages are, ahem, a cut above. I suggested the stables and this poor lady collapsed at my very feet."

Mary Rose hurried forward to take the other woman's arm. "You are very pale. Come sit down. I don't know what my husband is thinking by keeping you at the door."

Josiah's voice was loud and pleased. "A lady killer. That's what Jackson called me. She dropped right at my feet," he said again, and chuckled some more. "Jackson is likely telling one and all about how I rescued this damsel in distress. Well, all's well. I'm needed back at the factory. They will be talking about me throughout the town today." He set the bags down at the door, gave the women a short bow, and left.

Mary Rose led the other woman into her sitting room. "Rest here and I'll get some strong coffee and food for you."

Edwina sank to a chair and covered her face with her hands. "There has to be a way," she mumbled.

Exactly what Mary Rose had been thinking. Goodness, the day might not be so very dull, after all. She made the coffee extra strong and dawdled over the stove, giving the other woman time to recover her poise. By the time she returned with a tray, Edwina indeed appeared improved, though still wan. Loose strands of hair had been tidied and her shirtwaist tucked firmly into place. Dust dirtied the bottom of her skirts as though she had traveled hard and in the same clothes for days.

"You and your husband are very kind," the woman said. "I won't trouble you much longer, though I have to admit the coffee smells nice."

Mary Rose handed her a plate with bread spread with butter and a thick layer of currant jelly. The other woman nibbled at the bread and made appreciative noises.

"It's no trouble at all," said Mary Rose. She hoped for an interesting story to enliven her day and gossip about later. "You must have had a long journey. And if you are seeking a horse cart, a ways still to go?"

"I'm on my way to Colorado Springs," the woman said, eyes downcast and lips thinned. "I-I have kin there."

Mary Rose gripped the arm of her chair. Colorado Springs! "What a coincidence. My family is from that area. I don't recall anyone named Perkins. That must be your husband's name."

The woman blinked quickly and seemed to reach for words. "Yes. I mean no. I-I…" She rubbed her middle. "I do apologize. I'm terribly tired and I haven't felt right these last few days."

Mary Rose got to her feet. "I have just the thing. I'll be right back." She gestured to the plate. "Please have another piece of bread." She fetched the cure quickly, intrigued by this Mrs. Perkins and her trip to Colorado, a place very much on her mind lately.

As she reentered the room, she waggled a small brown bottle and held it out along with a spoon. The woman's unfocused gaze faced the window. "Mrs.

Perkins," Mary Rose began, to no response. Was the woman also a little deaf? She spoke louder. "Mrs. Perkins." This time, the woman startled and shifted toward her. Mary Rose smiled. "Have you tried Callard's Sherbetine? Josiah swears by it. It's meant for stomach disorders, but perhaps it could help settle your constitution."

Edwina waved a dismissive hand. "I have my own cures with me. I'm afraid I don't hold with store-bought medicines. I prefer natural herbs. My husband—" She stopped abruptly as though a thought struck her dumb, but then continued in a strained voice, "My husband calls my knowledge of plants and my ability to create tonics my only talents."

Mary Rose lowered the bottle and retook her seat. "My mother also believes in natural cures. She's a wonder when it comes to plants and herbs." Her tone grew more earnest as she spoke about her mother. "I haven't heard from her of late. She lives near Colorado Springs, right where you're going."

The other woman's gaze slid away and she didn't speak. An idea struck Mary Rose, so perfect it caused her voice to shake. "Perhaps you could take a letter to her for me. At least drop it by the city's post office. I've wondered at times whether my letters have even gotten that far, or whether they were lost."

Tears pooled in Edwina's eyes as she shook her head. "I'm sorry, really, terribly sorry. I haven't been truthful. And you and your husband are so kind. I'm not going to Colorado Springs at all. I—oh, what a mess I'm in." She lowered her head in her hands with a sob.

Oh my, what troubles this woman had. How terrible that Josiah refused to supply her with a wagon.

But…why lie about where she was going? Disappointment twisted in her heart as realization sank in that Edwina couldn't assist with a letter. Pity shifted to annoyance. Her hopes had been raised only to be dashed away. What game was this woman playing?

Sympathy waning, her voice tightened. "Perhaps I can help."

The woman swiped at her eyes with the heels of her hands. "I must head west, but my reasons are of a highly personal nature. I should go now and find a horse cart to buy. I cannot delay." Edwina rose. She swayed and sat down hard.

Mary Rose sized up the situation. Edwina Perkins had a few secrets and was desperate to leave town, and—unless this was also a lie—had knowledge of medicinal plants. *Recognize opportunity when it knocks*, her mother always preached. Yes, but she would need to tread carefully, assess the level of desperation and then strike. Risky, but freedom loomed.

"Rest a few more minutes," she said. "We happen to have a horse and cart that I may be able to sell to you, or trade, for a reasonable price." She leaned forward. "First, you must tell me everything. Then I will tell you my price. If conditions are met, you could be on your way within the hour."

The other woman gasped as she sat straighter in her chair. Her fingers wound around the fabric of her dusty skirts. She stuttered a reply. "I need your-your promise you will keep-keep my secrets."

"I promise." Mary Rose gave an encouraging smile. "We women need to stick together, don't we?"

The other woman's lips trembled. "My name isn't Edwina Perkins. It's Clara Walker." She closed her eyes as though in prayer, and the words raced out in gulping bursts. "They say I...my husband...but I-I promise I did nothing wrong. No one believes me. I must get away...a hanging judge...I must go...please help." She sagged in the chair as though exhausted by this confession.

Mary Rose fought back a hoot of triumph. Desperation oozed from the woman's pores. Clara Walker's situation was dire enough to do her bidding. Serendipity had transported this woman to her door.

Mother, you will be so proud of your clever daughter.

Chapter Three
Emma

Snap.

Emma Bailey cracked open one eye, every nerve on edge. The wind was up. Perhaps that's what stirred the horses and caused them to stomp and snort. Branches swayed in the moonlight. Ever so slowly, she shifted on her bedroll near the campfire's embers, just enough to take in her two prized horses and pack mule at the edge of the clearing.

Honor, the big black four-year-old with a deep chest, tossed his head and tugged on the tether line. He was her favorite—spirited, dependable and loyal. Faith, the yearling bay at his side, skittered sideways as though a rattlesnake were underfoot. She was still rough under the saddle; Emma knew to stay well away from her hooves. Faith was likely to bite and kick one day, and the next act as sweet as an angel. Only Gray, the mule, stood his ground; little bothered the sturdy creature except irregular meals. He'd been known to stop dead in his tracks if he felt a day's work had gone on long enough without an adequate feed in return.

Across the campfire's glow, a light rustle of last year's leaves drew her attention. There, a shadow. No, there were two. The hair on her arms stood up. She edged one hand to the pistol under her blanket. She'd be damned if horse thieves would steal her hard-won animals. Not to mention, their loss would leave her stranded midway through her journey, somewhere on the western edge of Oklahoma—harsh, unforgiving country. This was no place for a woman alone, and especially without swift transport.

She lifted the pistol to the edge of her blanket. No use blasting holes through it. Money was limited and she had a long way to go. Another two months, most likely the end of summer, until she reached Oregon and tasted the salty water at the mouth of the Columbia River.

No additional forms crept by the edge of her campsite. Two then. She prayed they weren't from a local tribe. Shooting one Indian meant hundreds would be clamoring after her scalp by morning. White men, though, were more likely. Newspapers bragged the Wild West was settled, and the Indian Wars pretty much over. Any natives still around were broken-down shadows of their former selves. Lands taken, homes burned, young men slaughtered.

Snap. Whispers hissed through the air. English. They were white men. Still dangerous as snakes out here in this wilderness where no eyes or law observed. Disposed to steal horses, rape or maim. Shoot and run? Call out a warning and hope for the best? If there was anything Emma understood, only fools relied on hope. She squinted, aimed, and shot.

****

For days after that, she scarcely slept. The horses wanted to run, to stretch those long, slender legs in flight away from the pistol's thunderous cracks, and the sharp scent of blood. Gray had one speed, however; a slow, plodding pace that promised to outlast all of them in the end. Emma trusted the mule's solid sense. Eat, rest, live. She tied the horses behind the mule and then lashed her hands to Honor's saddle while she rode. In this way, while she dozed, she was unlikely to break her neck in a fall. Somehow, Gray understood her terror—that people might make chase. He kept moving forward until the sun touched the horizon with a blaze of pink and the sky deepened to purple.

Sagebrush, boulders bigger than a house, deer darting from their path, a deep roll of thunder that threatened rain but never delivered. Three days after she killed the two men, the mule raised his head and, for once, quickened his pace. Emma woke and steered them away from the town—a stable with straw, warm oats to eat—that must be near. There was a tussle with the mule, but Gray was loyal too, and he lowered his head, set back his ears, and obeyed her command. "No towns," she ordered. "Bad." These events made a blurry impression.

On the seventh day, she fell into a river as they crossed. She had stopped tying her hands to the saddle but dozed off midday as nights brought intermittent sleep. Every hoot of an owl or small animal rustling the brush set her heart pounding. The drop from Honor's height, the shock of cold water, the instant awakening shocked her to her senses. She scrambled on the rocky bottom and raised a splash that sent the horses and mule lurching to the far bank.

"Stop!" she gasped, but the animals took off in a trot. "Oh shit!"

She fought her way through the water and emerged with hair dripping and her men's trousers and shirt drenched. The animals and all her worldly goods were gone. She shivered.

"Gray! Honor!" She didn't bother calling for Faith, as the young bay rarely responded to her name. The yearling needed plenty more training before she'd fetch top price. But the trail was a poor place for instruction and guidance. She'd planned to stop and train Faith at intervals along the way in order to demand the highest price for her by the time they arrived at their destination by the sea.

She headed in the direction Honor, in the lead position, fled. Fortunately, the three were roped together so they couldn't scatter. And Gray, in the rear, wasn't likely to tolerate a quick pace for long.

Twenty minutes later, she stumbled upon the horses and mule nibbling sweet clover in a clearing between a stand of leafy cottonwood trees. Honor raised his handsome head and his ears twitched in greeting. Faith and Gray didn't acknowledge her arrival, but kept their noses lowered in the delicate fodder. Bees went about their business among the wildflowers, and yellow-winged finches fluttered in the trees' lower branches. A red-headed woodpecker, its body speckled gray and black, tapped a rhythm on a trunk. A small creek gurgled, likely heading for the river that soaked her through and through. The peacefulness of the moment swept over her. Emma assessed the small meadow and their situation. They needed a rest from the journey, and this was the perfect spot to work the yearling for a few days.

She scratched the mule between his ears. "Good boy." She stripped her wet attire and donned her only spare set of clothing; the past months taught her to travel light. Then she began the work of unloading the packs and setting up camp.

Once stopped, it was easy to delay departure. One reason after another came to mind. Faith's training progressed well. They required some respite, and her behind and back ached from long days in the saddle. She set snares for squirrels and rabbits and bathed herself and the horses in the creek. Gray refused the indignity of a bath, but he let her wipe the dust from his eyelashes and ears. She halted in her tracks from time to time, recalling the sharp scent of gunpowder, crimson spreading from the horse thieves' upper torsos, their blank, unseeing eyes. Soreness and regret spread in her chest, where a tender heart used to be and now sat a sharp-edged stone.

Each afternoon, she rode Honor out to scout the terrain. A small town lay about an hour to the west. She assessed the place from a distance, behind a rocky outcropping. Four or five buildings on what held for a main street, bracketed by a church and a saloon. Men and women strolled in and out of unpainted storefronts. A series of simple cabins clustered together behind the church. Everything had the appearance of newness. Even the scent of sawn wood drifted on the air.

The river flowed through here too and must have been the reason town elders chose this place for their settlement. The whole valley pitched on a slight slope to the river, except for a flat spot where the community sat, perhaps fifty yards from the wide stretch of water. From Emma's perspective, the buildings lay in the river's path. One future spring, a heavy snowmelt would sweep the valley clean of its inhabitants. These people must be from somewhere dry.

Or they were witless.

Apprehension kept her away, but lack of supplies and perhaps a thirst to see others drew her back to the outcropping the next day, and the next. Each time, she never drew closer—the battle waging equal between fear and food. People meant supplies. People meant loss.

The sixth day at her meadow camp, she inventoried her remaining supplies. Three days of emergency oats for the animals if grass dried up. Two days of hard rations for her. If the snares stopped harvesting critters, she'd be forced to use precious bullets on sustenance.

She swallowed the bile rising in her throat. *Tomorrow, I will go to town.*

****

Emma squatted in the trees twice before setting out, her stomach in full rebellion. The small meadow glistened with morning dew and bees hummed from flower to flower. Gray basked in a patch of warm sunlight and his hooded eyes tracked their departure.

Honor's reins were slick in her hands as they passed the rocky outcropping and headed down the slope toward town. She fingered the swatch of black lace in one pocket, a bitter memento of the person she used to be—and a reminder of who she was now. A bell from the church rang as they drew near. Sunday. Somewhere, days had lost their meaning, but for some reason it was nice to know. Like little ants disappearing into their hole, townspeople headed to the church door and filed inside. Her arrival at the other end of the street apparently unnoticed, or of lesser importance than the weekly sermon.

The question begged: Were these settlers so unconcerned about strangers wandering into their town?

Or had they already spied on her as she did them, and deemed her harmless? In any case, as the bell's peal ended and its echo against the mountains faded, there was only the sound of muted voices raised in a hymn to greet her.

She tied Honor at the mercantile and surveyed her surroundings again. A grizzled man of uncertain age sat still as a rock upon a bench three storefronts down, poker-faced as he regarded her. Her heart fluttered as she gave him a quick nod and then stepped up on the boardwalk. Bad luck that she arrived on a Sunday when stores were closed. She gazed in the mercantile window anyway. The dusty glass gave her likeness a ghost-like appearance. The last time she saw her reflection was months ago. Before the fire. A prickle ran down her back. Then, so many months ago, a spotless mirror showed a girl in full bloom, rosy-cheeked, with mischievous eyes, dark hair tied back and allowed to cascade down in ringlets. Her first real gown, a cream taffeta with satin bluebells sewn on to the bottom, the waist clinging tight above complicated drapes of fabric. The whole creation so heavy she was out of breath before the dancing began.

Flames consumed the promise that image held. The person staring back now wasn't a phoenix rising from the ashes. Nothing that pretty. Thin face swallowed by cheekbones, wide gray eyes and a hard-set mouth that no longer recalled how to smile. Stained brown pants held up by a braided leather belt, and a blue long-sleeved shirt tucked in tight. A battered cowboy hat, found near a graveyard two months ago, covered her hair. Her pistol holstered on one hip.

She blinked and broke the spell. No time to gawk

at herself. A shadow shifted within and, hopeful, she tried the door. A bell hung above announced her entry with a merry jangle. A scrawny man, beard unruly, emerged from a back doorway. His gaze devoured her bit by bit. She scrutinized him in return, chin up so he wouldn't think her afraid.

He broke the silence with a chuckle. "Wearing your father's britches today, are ya?"

"No." She cleared her throat, unused to conversation. She sought something more to say. Something pleasant. "Good Sunday morning to you."

"It's Wednesday." He cackled. "Where you from, girl? The hills?"

"I've been traveling." She gestured toward the window. "I heard the church bell and saw people going inside."

"Funeral," he said in a clipped tone. "Pastor died, so I don't know who's holding the service."

"Ah. I suppose anyone can say a prayer."

Shelves rose high to the ceiling, too well stocked for a remote location. A larger town couldn't be too far away. An image of Faith and Gray grazing unattended in the small meadow rose in her mind. Anyone might come upon them while she was standing here practicing social niceties with this fellow.

"I require some supplies," she said. "Oats for my horse. Jerky, flour, cornmeal, dried beans, a few eggs if you have them."

He jerked his head in a nod. "I have 'em. As long as you have the coin to pay."

"I can pay."

He hustled around the store, gathering the items as she investigated further. A jar of honey, leather boots, baking powder. A book, *Twenty Thousand Leagues Under the Sea* by Jules Verne. She stroked the pristine cover, bent close to inhale the clean inky scent, and considered. A luxury, both in money and added weight to carry. But, oh, an adventure novel would be such a delight as days grew longer and evenings stretched out like warm taffy. She bit her lip and then added it to the pile on the counter.

"Mrs. Reynolds sews ladies' garments, just across the way," the proprietor said after she paid. "Funeral should be about done, and she'll be back. Just in case you're needing more delicate items."

"Thank you, sir. I'll be on my way." She hefted the packages, judging the bulky weight to be about twenty pounds, glad Honor tolerated larger saddlebags. Too bad she couldn't keep him. They had forged a bond during this journey.

"You have a happy Sunday." The man's chuckle followed her out the door.

She halted just outside. Two men stood near Honor's head. Both wore pistols but had friendly expressions. She took a deep breath and strode forward, lifted the saddlebag flaps and started shoving packages inside.

One of the men, clean-shaven and dressed for a funeral, whistled low. A whiff of tobacco wafted toward her. "He's a beauty. Must be sixteen hands." He assessed her. "Your daddy's horse?"

Emma hurried even while she sought to appear unconcerned. "Sixteen and a half hands. And he's mine."

"That's a lot of horse for a woman. How do you even mount him, if you pardon the phrase?" One side of his lip twisted up. The other man, with heavy sideburns and a thick tie loose at his neck, grinned widely at his friend's wit. A black gap where a front tooth should be.

"Best stand back." She untied the reins from the post. Honor's neck quivered and his long legs danced. The hooves sliced into the dirt, raising a small dust cloud.

"Holy Mother of God, that's a beast," sideburns muttered.

The men backed up, mouths agape. In one fluid movement, she seized the saddle horn, leapt into the stirrup and onto Honor's back. The horse backed up and swung his head sideways, nearly hitting one of the men. At the other end of the street, the church disgorged the mourners. They spilled in her direction. Emma nudged Honor into a trot and they left town unscathed.

*****

Now that people knew of her, it was time to break camp and travel onward. She busied herself that afternoon with repacking. She filled her canteens, tripped all the snares, and by the time the sun tilted far in the western sky, she was content they could leave at first light. The lazy week in the meadow had done wonders for Faith. The spirited yearling still nipped but not as regularly, and even responded to her name more often than not. Emma reminded herself the horses had been through trauma too. She'd gotten a bit snappish herself.

Faith followed the lead off the meadow like a puppy, and even nuzzled her shoulder as she tied the horse near the fire ring. She gave the usual low whistle for Gray, but the mule had found a rich patch of clover and ignored the call. With a sigh, she headed toward him, passing Honor on the way. The big horse snorted and nostrils flared. On alert, Emma scanned the grass for rattlers and then the tree line for bobcats or bear. Wolves terrified her, but so far none made an appearance.

"What is it?" she murmured at the horse's side as Honor's ears flickered.

Then a woman's high peevish voice carried into the clearing. "I don't think you know the way."

Emma froze. Her pistol was more than a dozen yards away in her bedroll. A greenhorn's mistake. She should have *known* they would come for her.

"Well, I've never come this way before, have I?" A second woman's voice, somewhat nasal, more than a bit annoyed retorted.

The heavy crunch and squeak of wheels announced the approach of a wagon. Emma dashed for her weapon. The argument continued as the covered wagon rolled into view.

"Is this even north? I do believe we've gone in a circle," the first voice, brittle in tone sounded.

"If we've spun full around, then we're still going north," the second voice snapped, beleaguered.

Emma stood, legs apart, one hand on the pistol at her hip. The covered wagon was old, the type used years ago by pioneers, before trains tamed the prairie, and they still lumbered across areas where tracks hadn't been laid. Two women sat side-by-side, too focused on their argument to yet notice the camp they entered. Their one horse, overmatched by the heavy wagon, was damp with sweat, its mouth flecked with froth.

"We should have stayed on the main road." The peevish one appeared much younger, curly gold hair topped by a large straw hat. She wore a light-yellow dress with lace at her wrists and throat, a perfectly inadequate outfit for travel. "Someone could have provided directions."

The older woman had finely-drawn features; a few strands of gray threaded through uncovered dark hair. Dressed in sensible blue calico, she gripped the reins too tight and the poor horse gave a pathetic shake of its head. "The whole point was to avoid people."

Emma strode forward and seized the reins. "For God's sake, you're killing him."

The two women gaped as though they were staring at an apparition. The horse, released from harsh hands, lowered its head and halted. Its sides heaved as flies drank at its sweaty flanks.

"Whoever let you fools handle a horse should be whipped." Emma dropped one hand back to her pistol, tempted to dispatch the women to hell for their cruelty.

The two travelers spoke in tandem. "Who are you?" and "How dare you call me a fool?"

Emma crooned in the horse's ear, her expert fingers undoing the buckles at its shoulders and haunches. By the time the older woman had climbed to the ground, Emma had the horse unhitched and was leading it to the creek.

"That's our horse," cried the one in yellow. "Clara, what is that insane girl doing? She's stealing him."

Shoulders stiff, Emma halted. Turning, she pointed the pistol at the one with the lace-covered throat. "I'm no horse thief." She cocked the hammer. "Apologize."

Chapter Four
Clara

Clara raised one hand, as though asking a question. Her heart raced at the sight of a gun cocked and aimed. "Don't shoot her. Mary Rose's mouth natters faster than her brain. No reason for bloodshed."

When the pistol remained leveled at her companion, Clara twisted her neck toward the wagon and snapped, "For God's sake, apologize already."

"I didn't m-m-mean it," Mary Rose blathered. "I'm sure you don't intend to steal our horse."

The pistol lowered, though the young stranger's expression looked doubtful. "Your wagon is too heavy a burden. You keep going like this and your mare will be dead within the week."

Clara sighed and set her hands on her hips. "I told her half those things weren't necessary. They'd only slow us down. We won't get anywhere with a dead horse."

Mary Rose clambered off the wagon. "I left most everything behind. The china cabinet and chintz covered settee. My carved cherrywood bed. You're extraordinarily ungrateful, after all I did for you."

Clara bit her lip. The other woman, slender as a reed, had turned her back to them and was leading their sway-backed mare to the far side of the clearing. Two other horses—tall, sleek creatures, with coats that shone in the sunlight—eyed the newcomers. A fat mule grazed nearby, seemingly uninterested in the latest events.

With a glance over her shoulder at her traveling companion, Clara followed the presumptuous woman toward the sound of gurgling water. Hera, or Dolly, or perhaps Bonnie—that self-absorbed Mary Rose was unable to recall her own horse's name—had its nose in a creek. The stranger, not long past girlhood herself, stayed at the animal's shoulder and kept up a steady murmur.

"We meant no harm," Clara said, taking a quick peek at the holstered pistol. "Perhaps my friend might discard a few items and lighten the load. We're headed north, you see, for good. Consequently, she felt the need to take as much as possible."

The woman gave her a side-eyed glance. "The wagon alone is as much as the horse can bear. She's been sorely used and requires rest. You can stay here tonight. There's a little town close by where I'm sure you'll be more comfortable the next few days."

Clara stiffened. "Not a railroad town, I imagine. I believed we were away from the route."

"No rail. The place appears to be a new settlement. But I suspect there's a larger city nearby, if a railroad is what you seek. Your friend might be more comfortable in a salon car."

The possibility loomed that a telegram had already been sent to the stations, one from Missouri that warned: *Watch for a dark-haired woman of middling age. Wanted for murder.* Or, from Kansas: *Watch for a golden-haired young woman. Wanted for murder.*

No, they needed to avoid towns along the rails, so

no railcar for them.

They had enough food for another three weeks, the span of time she had estimated left in their journey. At the end, her brother, Marcus, would offer shelter and protection. His hog farm outside the town of Wylder in the Wyoming Territory would be a refuge, and far enough from Missouri to ensure her safety. Minnie Turner, her girlhood friend, might guess where she'd fled, but surely Minnie understood to keep this knowledge to herself. Her friend cast blame on her in the beginning, but as the situation escalated, had recanted her accusation. Still. The damage was done. And now, she'd truly fallen into evil company with Mary Rose.

"I'm Emma." The young woman interrupted her musings. Gray, intelligent eyes under long dark lashes gleamed out of an unlined face. She had a well-tanned, flawless complexion, slender neck and bony wrists. She appeared half starved, swallowed up by the men's clothing she wore, but vigorous just the same.

"I'm Clara." She instantly regretted her words. She should have said Edwina. Or another alias, instead of leaving a trail of breadcrumbs for trackers to discover.

Emma glanced through the thin layer of trees that provided a filtered view of the meadow. "Clara and Mary Rose," she murmured, as though committing the names to memory.

Of course. She had named her companion right away and already forfeited their chance to be anonymous. What a terrible outlaw she made.

The horse had drunk its fill. The mare's head was up and had her eye on the big stallion nearby. Across the meadow, the wagon rattled and Mary Rose's voice carped from inside. It didn't matter that no one was around to listen, the woman still prattled. Two long weeks of complaints and observations, reminiscences and ambitions. On and on about her mother, who lived in Colorado. Never a word about literature or current events. Neither had Mary Rose heard of, nor cared about, Mrs. Elizabeth Cady Stanton and the right of women to be men's equals. Clara had never met a more empty-headed woman.

Emma tied their mare to a stake in the meadow so it could graze. Then, with a display of indifference toward the two visitors in her midst, tended to her own camp. Clara sighed for her only companions: one woman too chatty and the other too terse.

As Clara strode to the swaying wagon, she called out, "You'll need to remove a couple of those trunks. We can't risk losing the horse."

Mary Rose popped her head out the back of the wagon. "It's my wagon. My horse. You're taking a stranger's word too much to heart."

Clara let the comment go about the horse and wagon, that by rights now belonged to her. "I suspect she knows more about their care than we do. Think what could happen if we became stuck miles from anywhere. What are you doing in there, anyway?"

Mary Rose climbed out of the back and wrinkled her nose. "Finding my rags. My bleeding is due any day and I don't want to be caught short. It's hard enough to stay clean in this wilderness without having to scrub out a bloodstain."

Placing one hand on the frame of the wagon, Clara peeked inside. A tumble of dresses, bonnets, petticoats, stockings, and shoes cluttered the interior. An escritoire, small chest of drawers, and rocking chair sat against the back while six large trunks filled with Mary Rose's precious belongings lined the two sides. Clara's two bags were submerged under the torrent.

"The chest has to go. And at least three of those trunks. If we're to make it to my brother's farm."

Why, oh why, had she offered to share her place of refuge with this woman? The answer arrived as quickly as the question: Guilt and distrust. If she kept an eye on Mary Rose, the empty-headed chatterbox couldn't disclose her whereabouts or bear witness against her.

"My mother gave me the chest as a wedding gift." Mary Rose's mouth hung open in disbelief, as though Clara asked her to cut off her arm and toss it to wolverines. "My clothes will get filthy and be crushed outside of the trunks." She shook her head. "I'm afraid the horse will have to endure. Perhaps if we went a bit faster, the trip would be over sooner."

Clara bit her tongue. The woman was hopeless. "Two trunks must go. At the very least. Leave the rocking chair as well. My brother will have a house full of furniture, I'm sure." She strode away to avoid Mary Rose's protest. To the trees to relieve herself and then settled on a warm sunlit boulder to enjoy the sensation of stillness after a full day of jolts and bumps in the wagon seat.

A huge gray squirrel bounced along a narrow tree limb and small birds, not much bigger than a butterfly, flitted in the leaves. The heavy scent of wildflowers amid the pines and aspens tickled her nose. The burble of water over rocks, insects clicking, the soft snuffle of the mare as she chewed knee-high grass. Regardless of the serenity, the apprehension that began almost a month ago with Walter's death hadn't eased. Minnie's exclamation still echoed in her mind: *Oh Clara, what have you done?*

No one arrived to arrest her, but a buzz of questions began. First, by the pastor and Mrs. Wilson. Next came the coroner, who insisted on a thorough inspection of the medicine cabinet and questioned her quite sharply about the herbs in the lower drawers. Suspicion, like a snowball, gathered heft and weight as it rolled along. Rumors, nasty and pointed, flew about town. The day after Walter's funeral, the sheriff—and elder in their church—stopped by. More questions, this time about their marriage, whether they had argued recently, why she had stopped attending church in the two weeks prior to her husband's death.

Minnie visited once, her eyes nervous and hands jumpy in her lap. *No time for tea today, thank you, I must be off soon.*

"You've known me nearly all my life," Clara had said, aware of the plea in her tone. "Tell them I'd never hurt a flea."

"It's just…you'd been so unhappy with Walter," Minnie replied, as she edged toward the door. "I mean, all that talk about *divorce*. I'm not the only one who knew about that. Walter told the pastor, whose wife lunches with the sheriff's cousin." She cleared her throat, one hand on the door handle. "Judge Henry Howe is scheduled to come through next month. You know, he's the judge who sent two women to the gallows last year. *Women.* He would try your case if…if the sheriff…I just wanted to let you know." Minnie escaped without a backward glance, hurrying away from the house as though the scent of murder had the ability to cling to her skirts and foul her own home.

Clara had caught the afternoon stage to Leavenworth, Kansas, hopped on the first train headed west. Two men followed her from one car to the next. She slipped off the train at the next station and, in a rush, ended up on a train south to Topeka. Heavens, what a big town, with so many rail lines she lost count. Steamboats and construction, buildings taller than two stories. Her head spun with anxiety and the noise did little to ease her apprehension of imminent arrest. In confusion, she boarded the wrong train and hid in the lavatory while the conductor traveled through the cars punching tickets. She darted out when they stopped in Williamsburg, and done with trains and rail stations, trekked overland two days to Emporia. When Josiah Culver had clutched her arm at his carriage factory, her fear and exhaustion led her to believe he was carting her to the gallows. She fainted.

Poor jovial Josiah, with a wife who wished him dead and no idea how to make it happen. Mary Rose had a wagon and horse—and a single request in return. *Weaken his heart. Just a little something to end my misery a year or two sooner than his natural death. He's not the compassionate person you believe him to be. You have no idea how I suffer.*

Time was her enemy. A horse and wagon was required to convey her farther from the hanging judge to the safety of the Wyoming Territory and her brother. *Use this, just a tiny amount once a week. He will weaken over time.* Powdered crabapple seeds. She handed a small packet to Mary Rose. The woman frowned at the thin paper envelope. *Is there something more, another potion, in case this one doesn't work?*

Anxious to get away, Clara gave her a few pinches of belladonna.

"Stay for dinner, rest tonight," Mary Rose insisted. "Leave in the morning."

She was at the woman's mercy, but the horse and cart was promised and paid for. Clara stayed, nerves on edge, but the aroma of lamb chops and leek soup set her mouth to watering.

The crazy woman must have dumped both packets in Josiah's soup. He was dead by dessert. Clara stared at the prone man in disbelief. Two dead men in her wake. A hooded hangman flashed through her mind.

Her reverie was interrupted by the sight of a trunk at the back edge of the covered wagon. An unladylike grunt and then the trunk tilted and hit the ground with a thud. A second trunk soon followed.

Mary Rose climbed down and, with hands on hips, surveyed the meadow. She lifted her skirts and picked her way across the tall grass to Clara's rock. "Are you happy now?" She gestured to Emma, who laid a fire thirty or so yards away. "I imagine that one will plunder my belongings the moment we leave. Likely her intent from the start."

"I don't think she's interested in your petticoats," Clara said.

Mary Rose leaned her back against the rock, gaze riveted on the stranger's movements. "Where's she from?"

"I didn't ask. She doesn't seem charmed by our company."

A sigh rose from the blonde head, a rush of air like a tea kettle starting to boil. "I hope your brother has better conversation than you." Mary Rose pushed off from the rock and started across the meadow toward the woman's camp.

Clara sat up straighter. This should be interesting. She contemplated following to save Mary Rose from probable death. But, no. An image of herself freed from Mary Rose flickered through her mind: The wagon emptied of all but two modest bags, quiet travel days filled with contemplation and time to repent her sins before she arrived in Wylder. Because while she hadn't killed Walter, she most certainly played a role in Josiah's death. Though the poor man's wife laced his dinner with enough poison to drop a bison, Clara supplied the ingredients with few protestations. Atone she must. Just as soon as they arrived in Wylder.

Mary Rose's curls bounced as she approached the other woman. From her perch, Clara observed the two in conversation, but the sound didn't carry. Emma struck a flint and smoke curled from the fire ring. Mary Rose said something, and the stranger shrugged, uttered something in return. Loneliness rolled up in Clara. She missed her afternoon chats with Minnie, despite her friend's betrayal. The companionship of the two women across the meadow drew her forward. Down off the rock, past the grazing mare, to the circle of stones around the fire. A small flame grew and snapped as it fed on pine needles and twigs.

Mary Rose gave her a victorious glance, as if to say: See, *this* is how it's done. "Emma hasn't worn a dress in months. Men's clothing every day. Pants and boots." She giggled. "Even their underclothes."

Emma stayed in a squat as the fire grew in substance. She poked at the blaze with a long stick and added several small branches. Flames leapt higher and reflected in her eyes. "They're much more comfortable and practical for the life I lead."

"Imagine the to-do I'd make, clad in trousers, split up my thighs to put my feminine region on display." Mary Rose tossed her curls, a pleased tilt to her mouth, as though such exposure held appeal.

Emma snorted and rose to her feet. "I doubt the horses notice."

Clara sought a more practical topic. "Have you traveled far?"

A wariness crept into the woman's expression. "Far enough, and a ways to go yet." She lapsed into silence.

Mary Rose shot Clara a mean look. "Let's have dinner together, shall we? We have plenty to share, and I brought a bottle of sweet sherry for a special occasion."

Clothing, furniture, trunks and now intoxicating spirits? What else weighed down the wagon and contributed to their horse's near demise?

Emma dusted off her hands on her trousers. "No spirits for me, thank you, but I can share a pan of corncakes. And blueberries picked yesterday."

A sociable dinner sounded fine. Clara considered their supplies. "We have a bit of smoked ham and—"

Mary Rose interrupted, "We can each have an egg. No more than one per day. Clara keeps us on soldiers' rations." She laughed. "She's quite a taskmaster."

"We need to make our supplies last," Clara protested in a low voice, jaw tight. How dare she complain. After all, one of them needed to consider practicalities.

Their camp hostess had stalked away and fiddled

with a rope that hung from a tall pine. In a moment, a large saddlebag lowered to the ground.

"Heavens, you must value your cornmeal very highly to hide it in a tree," Mary Rose said.

"This is grizzly territory and they have cubs to feed." Emma frowned at them, then lowered her head to rummage in one bag. "How much farther do you have to go? This region has more dangers than bears and not safe for inexperienced travelers. As I suggested, a train may best suit your situation."

Clara exchanged a warning glance with Mary Rose to not speak of "their situation."

Her ever-nattering companion spoke. "What direction do you go?"

Emma crooked her chin away from the creek. "West for now."

Mary Rose clapped her hands. "How wonderful. We can join forces. Three is safer than two. Anyway, I could use a friend more my age. Someone able to understand my passion for life."

Enough.

Not waiting to hear Emma's response, Clara stomped off to the wagon to fetch the smoked ham and three eggs. She would repent once they arrived in Wylder and attend church faithfully each Sunday from now until judgment day. Today, however, dark thoughts filled her soul.

Chapter Five
Mary Rose

Dust caked the hem of Mary Rose's saffron-yellow skirt and now smoke from the fire stung her eyes and parched her throat. Her stomach growled in anticipation of dinner. Mother would be proud of her strong, determined daughter. Even though Josiah, too, had turned out to be a complete loss. His bulging blank eyes, purple face and protruding tongue, along with the crash he made as he fell to the floor, sent her into a panic. Clara's overreaction—screeching they must flee—hadn't helped. If she had only stayed; a cannier solution would have resulted in a considerable widow's inheritance. Only the guilty bolted.

No matter. *I've taken the reins of my destiny.* She was young and unencumbered by children, thank goodness. No one need know of husbands previous to Josiah. A vivacious widow, ripe for the picking. By the right—and prosperous—man, of course. The next time she mustn't err.

"Did you say something?" Emma asked from across the flames, her head cocked to one side.

Mary Rose laughed to cover her confusion. What had she said aloud? "I've taken to talking to my dear deceased Josiah when alone. Goodness, don't worry. A grieving widow has her peculiarities."

A shadow crossed the woman's face. "My

sympathies." Her tone flattened. "Did he suffer?"

"Oh no, the end came quick." She proffered a sad smile. "He was quite a bit older than I am. A longtime family friend who…who required companionship in his waning years." Yes, that made a wholesome story and unlikely to frighten off future suitors.

Emma shook a healthy amount of cornmeal into a pan, added a pinch of salt and something that must be baking powder. Her hands worked the ingredients together quickly as though they had made the motions a thousand times. She mashed a few blueberries into the mixture and added a trickle of water.

The woman, dressed so oddly, still hadn't responded to her invitation to join them on their journey.

"Do say you'll travel with us, at least as far as Colorado Springs where my mother lives. I'm not certain of Clara's ability to get us there, and I could use a true companion. I'm certain you and I will become friends."

A crunch of sticks announced Clara's return. Her sour countenance indicated she'd heard the comment denouncing her skills. "Here are the eggs, a pan and some grease."

Mary Rose scanned Clara's handful. "What about the smoked ham?"

"Here as well, in my pocket. Don't trouble yourself to help."

"I didn't expect it required four hands to fetch so little."

Emma huffed an impatient breath. "You two must be relatives as you surely aren't friends."

Clara knelt and held the pan containing a gray

lump of grease over the fire. The grease melted into a clear puddle, releasing the aroma of beef fat, and she balanced the pan on two flat rocks. "We aren't accustomed to each other's ways is all."

The eggs, cracked one by one, spluttered in the hot grease, followed by a few shavings of ham. At Clara's side, Emma scraped up one large corncake and flipped it to the other side. The aroma of food set Mary Rose's mouth to watering.

"I don't have plates and utensils to offer you," Emma said. "You'll have to use your own."

Reluctant to leave the heady scent, Mary Rose hesitated, but Clara's lips pursed in that manner she had before making a snide comment. Mary Rose tromped to the wagon, where her clothes had been crushed to one side to uncover their traveling larder. Ugh. The journey was difficult enough without her dresses wrinkled and filthy. The urge to straighten her wardrobe vied with the aroma of dinner. She snatched out two plates and forks, hesitated, then grabbed the bottle of sherry.

Hands full, she filled her lungs with air. Her nose tickled from pollen, she sneezed. The sherry fell and the glass shattered on a rock. The sweet smell drifted up as the liquid seeped into the earth. She gasped and swiped at dots of brown that appeared on her skirt where the sherry splattered. The lace at one wrist brushed against the stain and colored a dingy brown. Her good-natured willingness to share the drink had gone awry, her dress now filthier than ever. Being nice didn't pay. With a rag and water from a jug, she scrubbed at the stains.

"Whatever are you doing?" Clara's sharp tone bit through her, her haughty nose sniffed the air. "Heavens, are you drinking?"

Mary Rose sighed and gestured to the broken bottle at her feet. The scold was to be her burden. "Leave me be. I'll bring the plates directly."

Clara grabbed the plates from the back of the wagon. "Dinner is ready whenever you can make it back." Her expression softened and she lingered. "It's been a long day and we are tired. Let's enjoy a good meal and be friends. All will be better in the morning."

A pang rose in Mary Rose's chest. "My mother always used to say that."

"Mine did, too."

For once, Clara seemed likeable, gentle and kind. She really wasn't so unattractive when she smiled.

Mary Rose stooped to gather up the glass and toss it to one side. "Is your mother still living?"

"Both my parents are gone. Typhoid fever took them and my youngest brother in '75."

A twinge of fear struck her. Had her own mother taken ill and died with no word sent? Is that why letters had stopped? No, Mary Rose had already dismissed this concern. "I believe you will get along well with my mother when we get to Colorado Springs."

Clara's brown eyes grew serious and her tone reproaching. "Going near a city is dangerous for us, for reasons you must understand. We must let time go by. Your mother would want you safe. We will continue to Wylder."

There was time yet to persuade her to detour to Colorado Springs. Mary Rose's gaze drifted to Emma, who—what nerve!—had a plate on her lap and was eating without them. She tossed the last shards of glass away from the wagon, wiped her hands on the rag, and picked up her skirts. "She's going to eat all three eggs and our ham if we don't hurry. Quick, fetch the plates."

The swish of grass behind her assured that Clara followed with the plates. Her stomach growled as the aroma of corncakes and ham tantalized her again. Quickly, she assessed the meal. Two eggs, most of the ham and corncakes still remained. She smiled with relief and twisted to take a plate and fork from Clara.

Emma offered no apology for not waiting. Manners sorely wanting, she sat in silence and finished her meal while they served up their own. Every so often, the stranger glanced up at them, as though curiosity got the best of her.

"You are welcome to the clothes I must leave behind," Mary Rose said in order to make conversation. "The cloth is of the best quality and really quite tragic to toss on the scrap heap." In truth, the two dresses and petticoat in one of the discarded trunks suffered several tears and required a skilled seamstress's attention. But she doubted the woman before her, in the most unbecoming attire, would be too choosy.

"Thank you, but I prefer my own apparel," Emma said. "Besides, I must travel light. Poor Gray already carries a heavy load."

Gray? Mary Rose glanced toward the animals. Must be the mule, a gloomy name. By the wagon, two trunks sat abandoned. She dug into her meal, mood unsettled. Gray was how she felt right now.

Pieces of her life lay in the dust. When would she be able to accumulate so many dresses again? Josiah had admired her small waist and neat bosom, and the way her hips swayed her skirts. The first few months, he lavished money on a new wardrobe for her, the likes of which she had never experienced before. Silks, satins, velvet, a dressing gown trimmed with rabbit fur. She recognized he reveled in showing off his young, pretty wife, and she made sure he was well rewarded in the bedroom. Treat your husband like a king in the bedchamber, her mother counseled, and you will reign over the house like a queen.

What good was any of this advice if the husband was poor, or abusive, or old? Three husbands dead, and little to show for any of her efforts. She might as well be a spinster. Although…her gaze darted to Clara, as though her traveling companion had the ability to read her musings…ten dollars were secreted in the lining of one of her handbags, along with a few pieces of jewelry. A five-piece silver service was buried among her petticoats. At least there were a few treasures.

The simple brass wedding band from her darling Patrick, worthless in coin, but of highest value in her heart. She hoped her first husband forgave her sin against him so they could live eternally in the hereafter. If he was made perfect in Heaven, he must understand she didn't have a choice but to serve him arsenic-laced tea.

Emma's soft voice broke through her musings. "I rode as early as I walked," she said, in conversation with Clara. "My father was head trainer at a fine stud farm in…uh…east of here. He sat me atop champions and led them around the training ring. I learned at his side—everything I know."

"How unusual," Clara said. "Your horses are so elegantly shaped. A different breed to those I've seen before. Are they from the farm? And how did you come to be here all alone?"

Mary Rose listened carefully. Who cared about the

beasts? The second question was more intriguing. No woman traveled alone unless she had secrets to hide from the world of men. Of this, she was certain.

Emma's lips twitched and thinned. "I don't have anyone. Not anymore." She rose, her plate in hand, and gestured to theirs. "I can clean up. You two must be tired."

Here was an opportunity to speak to the woman alone. Mary Rose smiled. "I'll help. You wash the dishes and I'll do the pans. Clara can rest tonight."

They walked to the creek together and knelt next to each other. Small rocks dug into Mary Rose's knees and dampness seeped into her skirt. A favorite dress ruined. Tomorrow, the lavender gray dress must suffice, the one with a nasty burn mark she planned to one day cover with rosettes. No point in wasting good quality gowns on mules, women, and wilderness.

She followed Emma's example of using sand to scour the dishes. The greasy pans were the more difficult chore. She ought to have offered to wash the dishes instead.

She glanced behind to make sure Clara was nowhere near enough to hear. "It's urgent I get to Colorado Springs. My friend isn't convinced. Do me a favor and join my cause."

Emma dried the plates and flatware on a rag and passed the cloth over for Mary Rose to use. "Your friend told me you are going to the Wyoming Territory where her brother lives."

"I have no interest in Wyoming. Colorado Springs has always been my aim. I must see my mother. She…she may need my help."

A small lie, but perhaps true.

"My business takes me neither to Colorado Springs, nor Wyoming."

Mary Rose lifted her chin. How rude to give such a curt response. "I suppose our mare may suffer as you say, because of her heavy load. There is no helping it. We all have our burdens in life. Though someone knowledgeable about horses, such as you, might give her the care she requires to survive the journey."

Emma's eyes widened and creases marked her forehead as she bit her lip. "I suppose, since we travel in the same direction tomorrow. I can see you through the day, at least, and make sure the mare is provided with rest and water."

Mary Rose lowered her head to her task and hid a smile. Offer a carrot and people opened their mouths.

****

The buzzing of a mosquito woke Mary Rose the next morning. She absently waved it away. Her heart soared. As soon as tomorrow, she might be home in Colorado Springs. Tomorrow! Or, she frowned, at least the end of the week. Every mountain looked the same. How did anyone criss-cross the continent? Emma appeared confident and well-traveled, however.

Mary Rose donned the same muddy, soiled, sherry-splattered dress from the day before—no point exposing another gown to unpleasant conditions. The lavender gray might still be altered with rosettes. Her journey was nearly over and she might find a way to return to this spot and collect her discarded belongings.

The other two women dawdled, chatting easily over a morning fire while they ate more corncakes with jam. Anticipation roiled Mary Rose's stomach so she only nibbled the edge of hers, eager to get going. Clara was on again about how women ought to be the same as men, and Emma appeared to feign agreement. Another day of this, how annoying. The sooner they arrived in Colorado Springs and parted ways, the better.

Finally, they finished their fare. Clara led the mare to the wagon, with Emma close behind.

"Emma will travel with us today," Clara said. "She has a map and compass. Isn't that wonderful?"

Mary Rose smiled, her triumph hidden. "How nice to have fresh company. I'm sure we'll be fast friends by nightfall."

Emma stroked the mare's neck and murmured in her ear.

Inspiration struck Mary Rose. "Your horses are fresh and much bigger than mine. Hitch them to our wagon, won't you?"

Emma's expression darkened, and for a moment Mary Rose expected the pistol to be raised on her again. What a quick temper the girl had.

Emma hunched her shoulders and glared at her. "My horses are not broken to a wagon and will *never* be used in that manner. We will pair your mare with Gray, my mule, though he might object. Have you emptied the wagon of the furniture yet?"

Protest rose to Mary Rose's lips but faded as she conceded defeat. She clambered into the back of the wagon and blinked rapidly at the unfairness of the world. She shoved and heaved the chest of drawers and escritoire to the back edge of the wagon. "Do help me. No need to smash these to the ground."

Emma assisted her in dragging the furniture from the wagon, its wheels squeaking as they were unburdened by the weight. Mary Rose wanted to clench her fists and scream at the sky at the sight of her fine property on the dewy grass. If all went well, however, she'd fetch everything by week's end.

Hands on hips, she faced Emma and forced her lips to curl into a smile.

"Satisfied?"

Chapter Six
Emma

Clatter and chatter.

The other two women promised to be the worst of travel companions. The fair one selfish and vapid, the older one embittered and fearful. After months of little but the sounds of nature—wind through the treetops, crackle of the night fire, birdcalls, occasional wolf howl—and only the horses to talk to, the human noise was grating and dissonant.

Still. They traveled rough territory and three were more imposing than one. Two extra pairs of hands and watchful eyes. Supplies to share. Emma had decided to keep watch over their mare to save the pitiable animal from further abuse. The benefits of companions might outweigh the detriments. If Clara and Mary Rose became troublesome, nothing bonded her to them.

Already, the younger woman had inveigled her into a deceit. Their direction was due west, which ought to land them at the outskirts of Colorado Springs within the next day or two, depending on the terrain and roads. Clara appeared to have a skewed sense of direction or trusted Emma's lead. There was most likely a reason the older woman, who appeared to be forty or so, chose to avoid people, but it was not her business.

Gray proclaimed his displeasure at the wagon traces with a series of brays that sent a flock of blackbirds aloft. Emma resorted to tying Honor and Faith to the rear of the wagon while she strode alongside the mule to encourage him forward. Her new cohorts sat side-by-side at the reins. The trouble she undertook was assuaged by the renewed sprightliness in their mare's step. The creature must be beyond fifteen years old, worked hard, its joints loosened with age. The animal had pluck, however, a characteristic that would perhaps help her survive these two silly women.

Within a half mile, the trusty mule settled to his task, and Emma mounted Honor to scout a path forward. They skirted wide of the nearby settlement and continued west. Wild turkeys ran across their path once—huge creatures that appeared too heavy to fly—and she itched to shoot one for their dinner. However, the crack of a gunshot might draw trouble. This was unfamiliar territory and another town might lay beyond the next hill.

The first day progressed without sign of other people, and they camped beside a modest-sized creek-fed lake. A simple line and a half hour of patience under a stand of rustling aspens netted her enough trout for their evening meal. In the background, the annoyed tones of the two women rose and fell as they continued their ceaseless feud. Human company, though taxing, was somehow comforting. People with whom to share a meal, say good morning to, and trade small pleasantries. Their mare grazed next to Gray, her rear bumping lightly against his shorter one.

Emma fried the fish over the fire, the savory aroma drawing the other two women with plates in hand. She found satisfaction in the way her traveling companions fell upon the food. Loneliness, long submerged, became recognizable as it surfaced and ebbed.

Mary Rose plucked a final morsel from her plate and licked her fingers. "Stay with us another day. This is the best meal since we left Emporia."

Clara darted Mary Rose an undefinable look.

"Emporia," Emma said. "Is Kansas where you're from?"

Clara stood and tugged at Mary Rose's arm. "Thank you for the meal. You caught the fish so we will clean up tonight."

Mary Rose yanked her arm away. "There's no harm in telling *her*. I lived in Emporia until my poor dear husband, Josiah, passed on. Now I'm on my way to family." She gave a laugh. "Don't mind Clara. She doesn't open up to strangers easily. But you are a friend now."

Clara gathered their plates and utensils without another word and strode to the stream. With a sigh, Mary Rose piled cups on the frying pan.

"She does seem troubled," Emma said. "Are you concerned about how she will get to Wyoming on her own?"

"Clara is all common sense and practicality." Mary Rose headed to the creek, adding over her shoulder, "I don't worry about her at all."

Mary Rose ought to be troubled. A twinge of unease unsettled Emma. The land north of Colorado Springs held pockets of civilization but dangers still abounded. What harm would it be to travel a day or so more with these women, see them safely down the road?

The two horse thieves entered her memory, and she shuddered. That moment called for a swift decision;

anyway, they might have killed her instead, or left her abandoned to die in the wilderness. If God existed in the heavens, he would judge her harshly. She'd face that moment when it arrived. For now, however, survival required every skill she possessed. Who could have predicted her childhood boyish pursuits of fishing, trapping, riding, and shooting might one day keep her alive? Her future trajectory had once been the same as most women: find a husband and produce a family.

The cream taffeta gown with satin bluebells flickered in her mind—a creation generously paid for by her father's employer, a reward for his loyal service. She was invited, not to one of the Parker family's elite society balls, but to a modest coming-home celebration of their oldest son who graduated Harvard. His strong curved jaw, tall stature, and confident laugh drew her eye. Gilbert Parker whirled her around the dance floor, one broad hand on the small of her back. Other girls, daughters of modest town tradespeople, appeared envious of his attentions toward her, and she felt like a caterpillar that had metamorphosed into a butterfly.

Two glasses of champagne transformed the world into a lovely blur. The third glass found her hand-in-hand outside with Gilbert who carried a candle-lit lantern. A breath of air to clear her head, he said, and she stumbled with him to the stables. He backed her against one stall and his warm, firm lips caressed hers. Her first kiss. She thought she'd float off the ground with happiness. Then the kisses became more urgent and she wriggled futilely to break his grasp. He dragged her to a stall and set the lantern in the straw.

Memories threatened to overwhelm her. By habit, one hand reached for the bit of black lace in her pocket and she rubbed it between her fingers. Soothed by the scrap from her past, she thrust the past aside and focused on Clara. A woman should not travel alone. Even in the company of Mary Rose, Clara was vulnerable, for the callous younger woman was all too willing to abandon her companion.

Wyoming. A meandering path West might throw off any pursuers. The detour north might serve a practical purpose. A small voice inside cautioned, *don't get involved*, and her resolve to help Clara wavered.

Yet, another day passed and then another and Emma continued to travel alongside in an unspoken agreement. She checked her compass, and then her map, each morning to be assured they headed into the Rockies. They followed one well-rutted road, then another, nodding a brief hello to a family piled into a wagon dressed in their Sunday best. Clara flicked the reins to hurry past, and Mary Rose complained a chat with other people would have been entertaining. Emma said nothing, glad not to have stopped. She glanced back to the other travelers several times before they disappeared from sight, and then breathed a sigh of relief.

On the next day of travel, Mary Rose grew more animated. Her voice heightened in pitch and words flew from her mouth like a willow warbler at sunup. Frown lines appeared on Clara's forehead as they followed the sun's descent. Several times she opened her mouth as though to speak, but the question didn't arise until late in the day.

"Surely, there's a trail north by now." She glanced at the afternoon sun. "Wylder must be much farther north. We've traveled directly toward the setting sun so can't have gone north at all." Clara pointed to the right. "I believe we ought to take the next road in that direction. We are terribly lost."

Mary Rose giggled and covered her mouth. "We will arrive at my mother's house within the hour. She lives on a farm outside Colorado Springs. Already, the terrain is familiar. I daresay we picnicked in these parts once."

Clara stiffened and her mouth rounded in horror. "You know we can't go into a city. We must get to Wylder. They will hunt for you here."

To get a better listen, Emma let Honor drift back a few paces toward the wagon. These women had pursuers, crucial information to know about her traveling companions. Neither appeared to be dangerous, with no guns nor any other weapons in sight. But their connection to each other struck her as peculiar. The younger one likely had a living husband in pursuit and not deceased at all. Mary Rose didn't appear to be the type to make a constant sort of wife.

An abandoned and angry husband was likely to carry a gun and charge in, accompanied by an armed friend. She should have asked a question or two before she agreed to travel with these women. Her pride in her own competence kept her mouth closed, but she hadn't reckoned they could invite danger her way.

"There is no one better for solid advice like my mother," said Mary Rose. "She will tell us what to do."

Clara heaved back on the reins and their nameless mare and Gray halted. The mule looked back over his shoulder as though in complaint of such unnecessarily rough treatment. "Do you understand nothing?" she asked, as if Mary Rose didn't possess a lick of sense—a not unlikely condition. "The train runs straight from Emporia to Colorado Springs. You talk of your mother so much, it will be the first place they search for you. They might already lie in wait for you to arrive." She glanced around as though expecting men to burst through the trees at any moment.

Mary Rose's eyes narrowed. "You don't need to stay. Drop me off and run along to your wild country with its savages and beasts. That's all you'll find to the north." She waved a hand in the air. "Take the horse and wagon. They're yours, as agreed."

The mare nuzzled the mule's shoulder. Emma slid off Honor's back. If they were going to stop and quarrel, she would water the animals. Gray held his head high, and Emma sensed he enjoyed having a female admirer next to him in the traces. The babble from the two women cut the air like a jagged knife as Emma toted water from the back of the wagon. The lovebirds hauling the wagon were first, then Honor, and finally Faith. She patted the young bay who had come along so far in training during their time in the meadow.

As the women's squabble continued, she cleared her throat. "Who is after you, exactly?"

The two traded glances and, for once, stopped exchanging barbs. A red-tailed hawk circled above and a light breeze cooled Emma's neck. Somewhere far off, a train whistle echoed. Her shoulders tightened. Trains meant towns. Towns meant people. These two were plenty.

Clara shook her head. "I won't go to Colorado Springs. No, I won't be forced to go back home."

"There are people, a husband perhaps, who follow you," Emma suggested, her throat tight.

"No husband. I-I'm a widow."

Clara twisted her face away. The loss must be very recent for her to be so upset. Mary Rose had also claimed to be a widow. Were their deceased husbands brothers? Was that the connection? What lie existed under the surface of their words?

Emma frowned, unsettled by the raw emotions of the two women and her own role in deceiving Clara about their destination. "I don't want trouble. I believe I'll take my mule and go my own way."

"There is no trouble," Mary Rose said loudly, and snatched the reins from Clara's hands. "She worries too much. Let's go a little farther. It will be evening soon, and you'll have to camp anyway. If you'd like, I can give you some of my mother's apricot preserves for the rest of your journey north. She's known all over the county for her jams."

If Gray weren't hitched to the wagon, Emma would say her goodbyes now. As Mary Rose didn't appear willing to let go of the reins, Emma would be forced to draw her pistol again. The gesture an empty threat as she dare not discharge the weapon so near a town, where a sheriff might hear the shot and choose to investigate.

Lips in a thin line, she mounted Honor. "A bit closer and then." She glared at Mary Rose. "You walk the rest of the way to your mother's house. Clara and I will camp outside of town while you make arrangements to fetch your belongings from the wagon."

Without waiting for Clara to agree, Mary Rose snapped the reins with a crack and the wagon jolted forward. What a relief to soon leave these two behind.

One more night.

****

They camped near a thicket of dense cottonwoods. The fluff released from the trees' pods floated on the air like a late spring snow shower. A log cabin sat alone on the other side of a low rise, surrounded by newly planted fields, the sprouts peeking just above rows of earth. Mary Rose exclaimed in joy at soon seeing her mother and had hurried toward her family's cabin as soon as the wagon rolled to a stop. Smoke drifted on the air from the distance, the unseen town fortunately too far away for spying eyes. With luck, their passage near Colorado Springs might go unnoticed.

Clara unhitched the animals without a word, her face white and grim. They set up camp in silence. As Emma lit a small fire, scrapes and screeches drew her attention to the wagon, where Clara had thrust the rest of Mary Rose's trunks to the ground.

Emma didn't want to care or get further involved, but Clara's wan expression begged a question. "Do you know how to get to Wylder?"

A tear rolled down Clara's cheek. "I suppose I must ask in town and then stay near the roads."

"Your brother…does he have family? A wife and children? Perhaps they won't mind your staying with them."

Clara sat on one of Mary Rose's trunks. "He's been too busy with his farming to find a wife." She frowned. "At least, the last I heard from him, he wasn't courting anyone. That letter was written more than a month ago. No matter. He will be happy to see me." A hesitation in the woman's tone belied her words.

The situation bothered Emma. Mary Rose had

discarded her companion so easily. Clara seemed ill-equipped to travel alone; even Mary Rose had better survival skills, or at least an innate sense for landing on her feet.

"I'm surprised he hasn't arranged to meet you, at least part way, to assist in your journey," Emma said. "You wrote to him, to let him know of your pending arrival?"

A false smile broke over Clara's face—her lips spread too wide. "Of course, of course."

The woman was a bad liar. Still, it wasn't her business. At dawn, they would travel in different directions—Clara north and Emma west. A twinge in her heart. Not pity, but concern for Clara. She mustn't be deflected from her goal. There wasn't anything for her in Wylder, Wyoming.

Mary Rose burst over the small hill, skirts hiked to her knees. Her face was red and tear-stained. "Hitch the wagon! Treachery! Scoundrels!"

Gray brayed his displeasure at being startled from a doze, and the horses snorted in anxiety. The hill behind Mary Rose was empty of pursuers, but Emma's hand trembled on the pistol at her hip.

Clara was on her feet, a hand pressed to her chest. "What's happened?"

"They say Mother is dead, although I'm certain that's a lie. They say the sheriff wants to speak to me, and they asked if I traveled alone." Mary Rose's tousled curls shook as she panted out this news. A tangerine ribbon hung loose atop her head.

Emma's heart flip-flopped in her chest. Surely, this silly woman hadn't told them her name. "Who says all this?"

Mary Rose pointed in the direction of the cabin, eyes wild. "The charlatans who live in my mother's house. The sheriff stopped by three days ago in search of me and with enough information and questions to wrap a noose around both our necks. They said my mother took ill after my marriage to Josiah. I knew I shouldn't have married him. He's showered such bad luck down on me!" She wrung her hands. "Get the horses."

At the mention of a sheriff, Emma whirled and busied herself with the animals while the other two women, heads close together, murmured and moaned. The mare and Gray needed rest, but now they must do double duty and help them flee the county. What had this silly woman told these locals? She might have put them all in peril.

Mary Rose, now aware of her trunks dumped from the wagon, had switched from fear to grievance. "Why are my belongings in the dirt? Help me load them up."

Clara fisted her hands on her hips. "We need to travel lighter. Those trunks are as heavy as boulders."

A cry emanated from Mary Rose, who had unlatched one trunk. "My china! All broken." She flew at the other woman, hands flapping and slapping. Clara raised her arms to ward off the blows.

The sight might have been absurd if not for the present danger. Emma seized Mary Rose by the waist and dragged her back. "Stop this behavior. Brawl later, if you must." She gripped the recalcitrant woman until she stopped her struggle. "Clara is right, the wagon is much too heavy. You must abandon it altogether. Even the most incompetent tracker will discover us by morning."

Both women protested the loss of their wagon and shelter. Too much time had already been wasted for more debate. Let them keep their myriad belongings and the unwieldy wagon. Emma strode away while Clara finished rehitching the mule and mare. Mary Rose emptied the bulky wooden trunks, tossing clothing from within pell-mell into the back of the wagon. Shoulders stiff, Emma saddled Honor and tethered Faith to a lead.

Their small party started off, due north toward the Wyoming Territory. As bothersome as the two women were, Emma didn't want them harmed. A frisson of curiosity rippled through her. The local sheriff had "enough information and questions to wrap a noose around their necks." She glanced over her shoulder at the two women side-by-side in the wagon. What terrible crime had they committed which would send them to the gallows?

Forgery? Perhaps arson?

Or…murder?

****

Despite the risk, they resorted to a road for their night flight. A quarter moon provided a glimmer of light to see by, and any nearby farmhouses lay behind at least an acre of land. No thunder of hoof beats trailed in their wake, no shouts for them to halt. Dark shapes fluttered and swooped as owls and bats emerged. Crickets chirruped and the scent of wet fields ranged over Emma. The stars rotated in the sky as the night moved forward.

She dozed, jerked awake several times, and was comforted to hear the steady crunch of wagon wheels and clip-clop of hooves. Stars winked out one by one, and a soft yellow showed in the east as dawn approached.

She glanced behind. Mary Rose and Clara both asleep, their heads on each other's shoulders. Mary Rose murmured as she dozed. Gray and the mare had their heads low, the reins loose on their backs. Such faithful creatures to soldier on through the night. A clearing showed beyond the trees, off the road, and she led the way through a gap just wide enough for the wagon. Around a bend, Emma dismounted with a groan, her numbed legs nearly giving way as her feet touched the ground. Her body ached from being too long in the saddle.

The bumpy terrain had jolted the slumberers from their dreams, and they too climbed down from the wagon grumbling at their discomfort.

"Let's get the animals fed and bedded down," Emma said. "We'll travel by dark for the next few days."

For once, no one argued. Mary Rose, pale with fatigue, stumbled to the trees for privacy, while they watered and fed the livestock. Too tired to eat, Emma laid out her bedroll next to a line that tethered Honor, Faith and Gray. If the sheriff arrived, she wanted an opportunity to escape with her animals. For now, she'd stay with these hapless women and assist their flight.

A low murmur of conversation rose and fell near the wagon interspersed with the click and hum of insects, and the shifting of the horses. The warmth of sun grazed her face and her limbs relaxed. Pistol at her side, she let herself sleep.

Chapter Seven
Clara

Due north, at last. The mountains soared above, emerald green and topped with patches of white, exactly as her brother wrote in his letters. Each mile drew them closer to his protection. With the unfortunate incident in Colorado Springs a week past, they again traveled in sunlight. Clara was grateful for this, as she grew up to believe the night air poisonous. Nothing Walter ever said convinced her otherwise, even though he'd been to medical school and read all those important journals. Sometimes, folk medicine and the old ways were best.

No sheriff or posse chased them, the people in Mary Rose's childhood home must not have exposed them. At least not right away. One thing she knew for certain, town folk were quick to take offense and call in the law. Country folk liked to mull things over a bit before they sought interference from outside.

A handful of travelers met them on the road. A family on their way to Denver; two Army officers mustering to Arizona over range wars there; a farmer who only grunted in response to their greeting. None of them had been to Wylder before, though the officers were familiar with Wyoming's capital, Cheyenne, a day's ride east of the town according to Marcus' letters. Their destination not more than ten days away, according to Emma's maps and compass, it took everything Clara had not to rush the mare and mule into a trot. She must be back in God's favor, for Him to help them escape the law so close behind them. A dozen times a day she offered up thanks and swore a renewed allegiance.

Mary Rose had grown quieter since receiving her shock. How tragic to discover her mother had died, and the farm lost to strangers. She remained pale and less argumentative. Emma had attached herself to them, which was fortunate since the mule took half the burden off the mare Clara dubbed Lucky.

This sparked the only disagreement of the week. "I doubt she feels lucky, hauling us around," Mary Rose grumbled. "How about something pretty, like Daisy or Matilda?"

Clara shook her head, firm on this subject which touched upon their shared crime. "As you like to remind me, I paid for Lucky fair and square. She's mine, so I get to name her."

Surprisingly, that remark ended the conversation. Mary Rose crawled inside the wagon for a two-hour nap, and Clara spent the time daydreaming about a new life in Wylder. Her old friend, Minnie Turner, used to say God required payment for answered prayers, just like a shrewd shopkeeper who collected debts with a firm hand. While the idea smacked of blasphemy, her current situation was proof of Minnie's theory. Hadn't she wished to be free of Walter? Didn't she long to see her brother once more? God delivered his end of the bargain; her current difficulties were the payment. She would prevail and repay the debt to Him with interest. It was ironic widowhood had filled her heart with gratitude and brought her back to the church's teachings.

That notion in mind, she clutched the reins and closed her eyes. "Dear God, I thank you for your continued blessings. You do work in mysterious ways." She cracked open one eye to make sure the wagon didn't veer off the road during her prayers. Ahead, Emma sat astride her leggy black horse, its slick and well-tended coat shining in the sun. The bay yearling pranced behind; a shade smaller and narrower in width, but also magnificent. Both horses were different—more elegant—than any she had seen before. By comparison, her mare appeared a broken-down nag. How had a young woman acquired such fine animals?

Both eyes open now, prayers set aside, she considered her newest companion. Men paid handsomely for first-rate horseflesh, and these animals were surely worth some money. The girl had said her father worked at a stud farm where champions were raised. Had she stolen two such champions? Horse stealing, especially ones so valuable, was a hanging offense. Good Lord, were all three of them barefaced sinners and hunted by the law?

A stouthearted brother and decent man, Marcus would protect her with his life. He'd know what to do about the too-talkative Mary Rose. Emma had her own destination in mind and might part from them at any time. Whatever would Minnie have made of her companions? Though Minnie's initial public suspicion cast doubt on her innocence, Clara missed her friend. They'd been together too many years for a permanent rift. Perhaps someday she could write to Minnie and they might grow close once more.

She drifted into another daydream, one in which future children played in a field. Twins, a girl and a boy. Towheads, like their future unseen father—a kind man, perhaps a widower with two other offspring. The children, now multiplied into four, turned and waved to her, their smiles wide and beautiful. She waved back, heart full.

Nothing was impossible.

****

Emma insisted on resting the horses for a day. They stopped by a small mountain lake, the water crystal clear. Clara stripped down to her knickers and camisole with a giggle at her brazenness and stuck a toe in the water. The cloudless sky allowed the sun to beat down its full mid-summer glory. Her bare shoulders burned even as her feet froze in the snow-fed lake. She couldn't recall the last time her heart beat so strongly and her mood so buoyant.

"Jump in," Emma called out from behind her. "I dare you."

Clara glanced over her shoulder where Emma baited a hook with grubs dug from a rotten tree stump. "The water's freezing. How can that be in the middle of July?"

The other woman frowned. "It's July?"

"Yes, of course. July fourteenth or fifteenth. I lost a day, I think. I like to keep track." Clara kicked up a spray of water and breathed in deeply. Seven weeks since Walter's sudden death. Seven weeks a widow. Not a miserable, wretched thing to be. Rather, a weight lifted from her neck. She hadn't wished him dead, not really. Only a divorce.

Emma picked her way down the rocky beach

several yards away and cast out a looping line, which she had tied to a short stick. Barefoot, with trousers rolled up to just below her knees, the young woman waded out into the water. She wasn't a stranger any longer, their rough travels and travails drawing them close.

"It's not so cold," Emma said, gazing out over the lake. "I may go for a swim later."

Clara suppressed a shiver. Her feet were already nearly numb. In the distance, snow topped impossibly high mountain peaks. Mid-July and still white-capped. They must be very close to Wylder now, but she dare not ask Emma yet again how much farther. The woman became ill-humored if pressed. Surely any day they ought to come upon the town. A frisson of excitement dashed through her. She waded in deeper, to her knees and then her thighs.

"Watch this!" she cried and launched herself toward the middle of the lake. She ducked under and blood rushed to her head. Her scalp tingled. She rose, gasping to the surface. Tears sprang from the cold and she scrambled to the shore. Water streamed off her knickers and her hair broke loose from its ties. A stranger's laugh startled her, and she searched for the source.

It was Emma, her solemn mien transformed into merriment. Eyes bright and mouth upturned. Heavens, the girl was lovely.

"You've scared all the fish to the other side of the lake," Emma said. "But it was worth it to see you go under. Whatever made you do it?"

"You dared me."

The sun felt delicious on her back and shoulders,

instantly warming her. She squeezed water from her clothes and hair. How many years, decades even, had it been since elation fluttered quite so in her chest? The uncommon sensation caught her by surprise.

Emma laughed again. "I never expected you to dive in. The water's much too cold."

Her eyebrows drew together as she yanked on the line then wrapped it quickly around the stick. A moment later a plump fish, silvery with flecks of pink on its belly, flopped onto the rocky shore. Emma threw it higher on the rocks behind her and baited the hook again. The frantic jerks of the fish lessened until it finally went still.

Clara sat on a large boulder nearby and leaned back on her elbows. What freedom there was in lounging outdoors in her knickers and camisole, no petticoats or heavy skirts about her legs. If she lived like Emma, how long until she wore trousers, too?

An eagle soared high above, tracing circles in the sky. Gazing heavenward, Clara combed her hair with her fingers. Though a few strands of gray invaded, her dark hair still fell thick and soft, a mane any man would enjoy burying his face into. With practiced movements, she wound her tresses and knotted a messy bun at her neck. *I might not be beautiful any longer, but attractive for thirty-six. And perhaps fertile.*

Across the lake an animal stepped forward to sip at the shore. An unwieldy rack of antlers on an oversized head appeared out of proportion with its gangly, nut-brown body. "What in God's name is that?" she asked Emma, who hauled in another fish.

"Moose. We'll see more of them in these parts, along with bighorn sheep and antelope, or so I've read."

She lowered her chin and focused on the water as her prey put up a fight. "They attract big predators, like wolves. Good thing you'll be off the trail soon."

The second fish flopped onto the rocks and Emma withdrew a long knife from a sheath at her side. She sliced each fish from neck to tail, not even wincing as she ripped innards out and slung them into the lake. The splash raised the moose's head in alarm. The animal stared at them for a long moment, then picked its way up into the trees and melted into the undergrowth.

So many wonders in this world, Clara thought.

Emma rinsed the disemboweled fish and stood. "Let's have lunch."

"Weren't you going in the water?"

Emma strode up the beach toward their camp. "I don't swim," she said over her shoulder, a laugh in her throat.

****

Mary Rose appeared briefly for lunch and then returned to the wagon for her second nap of the day. Melancholy must have set in. Compassion mixed with irritation about her companion. The woman might feel remorse over Josiah, especially now her mother was gone too. Should she suggest prayers and atonement? Perhaps when they arrived in Wylder, she'd convince Mary Rose to attend church with her. They could wash their sins clean together. If Clara conveyed another soul to God, perhaps He might forgive her sins more quickly.

Emma saddled the bay horse which had a skittish, obdurate nature, and took off in a gallop down the road. That the animal required training was an understatement. The previous day, Clara offered an apple core, and the mare nipped her forearm. Fortunately, only her sleeve tore, and no blood drawn.

Though the brief swim had been exhilarating, the day delay chafed at Clara. Mountains grew taller and more majestic the farther north they traveled. Surely, Wylder must be close now. The threat from behind seemed very distant. Weeks of travel placed hundreds of miles between Walter's grave and her. Any tracker worth his salt would have caught up to them. Anyway, the hanging judge must have left Platte County, Missouri, by now. She breathed easier, slept sounder, and hope swelled in her breast. Her meditations focused on Wylder, her new home. Many of the herbs in her satchel had seeds attached. She would plant a small healing garden and explore the flora of the area for more possibilities.

That plan propelled her into the woods nearby to scout native plants. With a small sack at her side, she dug up dandelions to aid digestion and gathered yarrow to ease fever. A cluster of small brown mushrooms on a rotted tree stump was unfamiliar. Using a stick, she tipped one to view its pale, ribbed underside. Some mushrooms were so deadly that even handling one could leave its poison on her fingers for hours. She left the fungus in its place, with no appetite for other harmful potions in her kit.

She worked her way in a wide circle around their camp, always keeping the wagon in sight through the trees for fear of getting lost. Dirt gathered under her fingernails, trees swayed above, birds called to one another. The air swirled with the scent of rotting plant matter and musty tree bark. Time elapsed, the only sense it passed was the sun's shifting place in the sky.

At the edge of her consciousness, she noted that the bay and Emma returned, and the woman headed toward the lake. Mary Rose clambered from the wagon and aimed toward the spot they agreed on for a privy. No one appeared to care she was gone. Finally, her bag a satisfying heft from gathered treasures, she prepared to see about dinner.

A light splash drew her attention in the lake's direction. Emma had headed that way earlier, but the woman asserted she didn't swim. The horses and mule clustered together under a tree, and again, Mary Rose appeared to fiddle with clothes in the wagon. Who or what made that sound? Her heart increased its tempo. A bear or, God forbid, a wolf? Did they even swim?

With trepidation, she crept to the tree line at the edge of the shore. Yards away from shore Emma's head and bare shoulders rose above the frigid water as she swam toward the beach. She had lied about not being able to swim. How peculiar. A pile of clothing lay on the rocks—shirt, underclothes, trousers with a piece of black lace peeking from a pocket. Clara glanced startled back at the lake and instinctively surveyed the shoreline for any other people. Unclothed! She shrank behind a tree and leaned against the trunk.

Splashes drew her attention back to the water despite her astonishment. In eighteen years, Walter had never seen her completely bare. They conducted nighttime activities with the candles snuffed; bathing was always a once-a-month solitary endeavor.

Emma rose from the water, rubbing her arms briskly. Without clothes, the young woman appeared gaunt, hipbones and ribs prominent. Pity overtook Clara. So capable in many ways but Emma didn't know how to care for herself. If she and Walter had a child in the early years of their marriage, a daughter might be near Emma's age now. It wasn't uncommon for women in their thirties to be grandmothers. A pang of caring swept through her. *This* is what being a mother felt like.

Emma bent down to retrieve her clothes and then faced the lake to dress. Clara gasped and clapped a hand over her mouth. Puckered red scars covered one hip and down the back of one of the girl's thighs, hideous to observe. Clara leaned against the tree, out of sight. No wonder Emma desired privacy to swim. The burn scars—for Clara had seen such scars before, though never so substantial—appeared recently healed and must have been excruciating to suffer. The cold lake likely soothed the skin.

A crack near her head made her jump. Emma stalked past her and hurled away a stick apparently smacked against the tree. Clara's face grew warm at being caught spying. She bit her lip and hurried back to camp.

"Emma, I didn't know—I'm so sorry to have—" Oh, what was she trying to say? "I may have something to ease the healing. Of your burns."

Emma's glower could have flayed skin. "Leave me be. I don't require help."

"But how—"

"See to your own business, not mine." The words came clipped and harsh. Emma jutted her chin toward the wagon. "You have enough problems as it is."

Clara followed her gaze. Mary Rose fussed among her belongings. Dresses laid out, either to air or loosen wrinkles. Lavender, yellow, crimson, emerald—a constellation of hues overlapping like a spring bouquet.

Ivory corsets hung on the wagon's side, along with snowy petticoats. Three different sized bustles lay on a rock nearby. Clara knew no one with so many clothes and made with such fine fabrics. She had always considered herself wealthy enough with five dresses— three simple calicos for everyday use, a modest charcoal for church, and an old navy, threadbare at the hem and cuffs, for cleaning the stove or other grimy chores.

With Mary Rose's mother dead, the blonde woman had nowhere else to go except to Wylder. Clara knew her brother, always kind in words and deeds, would welcome a visitor for a short term, but nothing permanent. Clara was family, Mary Rose not even a friend. Not really. What if Mary Rose ever told Marcus about the belladonna? Her stomach did a somersault. But, of course, any such revelation cast blame on both of them. Mary Rose understood to keep quiet on this score.

Emma stomped off toward Honor, a saddle and bridle in her arms. She stroked the elegant animal's neck and back, and it nuzzled her hair. In minutes, she mounted and rode off through the trees.

Secrets, Clara thought.

****

Dinner became a quiet affair, with each of them lost in their own musings. The ham was long gone, as were the eggs. They dined on corncakes, beans and a can of peaches.

Mary Rose scraped her plate clean. "We ought to open one more can tonight. Next town we come to, we must get more food. I simply cannot eat another corncake."

Clara gathered the dirty dishes and laid them in a pile. She refused to consider another delay, another roundabout route to lengthen their journey. "Our food stores are very low, but I believe we can manage until we attain our destination. Especially since Emma is so very adept with her snares and fishing lines."

"My body craves a more varied diet." Mary Rose sighed, and her expression softened into something dreamy. "Fresh yeast rolls with butter. Roast mutton. Sausages and fried potatoes. A rhubarb pie." Her throat worked as she swallowed.

"Every stop makes our time on the road longer." Clara sought Emma's support with a glance. "We've been very fortunate not to have fallen ill or suffer disaster. Let us finish our journey quickly now that it's near the end."

Emma cleared her throat. She had been quieter than usual and avoided Clara's eye since the scene at the lake. "I met a man and his wife about a mile from here, while I was out on my ride. They have a ranch, where they raise cattle and sheep."

Hope leaped in Clara's heart. "Did you ask them if they're familiar with Wylder?"

Emma shook her head. "I didn't need to. They volunteered that they live near there."

Clara jumped to her feet, knocking the dishes over. "My goodness, they must know my brother as he's lived in these parts for ten years. He has a hog farm, a very nice one from what he's said in his letters. What is their name, this couple, so I can tell Marcus when we arrive?"

Mary Rose tugged at her elbow. "Let her speak. We've heard plenty about your brother and his *very nice* hog farm, and nothing about these people Emma met this very afternoon."

Emma paused a moment, as though to make sure another outburst didn't loom. She then nodded her chin toward the road. "They said forty miles, no more. We'll make Wylder in two, three days at most."

Chapter Eight
Mary Rose

Mary Rose leaned over and heaved the contents of her breakfast, making sure none of the sour mess splattered her skirts. Insides emptied, throat raw with retching, she braced herself against a pine tree with one hand. Her bleeding should have started more than two weeks ago. There was no doubt anymore.

Damn Josiah. Damn all men.

She was sure Emma suspected. The young woman's gaze had a piercing quality that quite unnerved her. Clara, not the brightest of females though book-read and with opinions aplenty, had no idea.

Well, she'd suffered two miscarriages during her first marriage. Perhaps there would be a third. Her heart twinged, grieved at the prospect, and she firmed her shoulders. Really, that would be a blessing for the unborn child. No father to protect it, a mother with no home. Men wanted their own offspring, not the leftovers from a previous husband. If a miscarriage occurred, she mustn't allow herself to mourn. A husband, a respectable one, *must* come first. Pregnancy gave women an unnatural appearance—all puffy and misshapen—and then a yowling creature slithered out amid blood and pain. Next came broadened hips, saggy breasts, and old age. No one would marry her then. Marriage was the only way forward. No other option existed for a proper life.

She had witnessed poverty first-hand. A woman's privation was far worse than a man's. A desperate female fell prey to scoundrels and ruin. Hunger drove many a woman into depravity—for what else did she possess but her charms? She must harden her mind and secure a suitable husband soon, at any cost.

Mary Rose spat and wiped her mouth. Another day of rocking atop the wagon filled her with aimless rage. She longed for a town, clean sheets, a boardwalk under her feet instead of dirt, a proper carriage, a milliner's shop, a coal stove, a hot bath, and—oh—interesting people to talk to and about! She kicked a rock on her way to the clearing and winced at the resulting pain in her toe.

Clara's expression showed concern from her place on the wagon's seat. "Are you well today, Mary Rose?"

"Yes, thank you. My constitution is unused to this type of life." She scowled as she ascended to the wagon's seat. She arranged her dark gray skirts and, with a grimace, tucked a wet spot behind her leg. "Josiah called me his hot-house flower. I'll never be a wildflower."

"Very poetic, your deceased husband," Clara said in a flat tone.

Mary Rose stared at her. Was she being mocked?

Clara snapped the reins and the horse and mule leaned into their harness. The wagon lurched forward, Emma seated on Honor about twenty yards in front, with Faith at her side. Clara's face broke into a smile. "We'll surely arrive in Wylder today. Can you believe we made it this far with so little trouble?"

Mary Rose fought to calm her voice. "Do you

forget I've lost both my childhood home and mother? You, at least, have family to take you in. I have nothing."

The woman's smile faded. "Forgive me, I didn't mean to be unkind. I noticed you wore mourning today, however belatedly as a widow, and should have chosen my words more carefully."

Mary Rose dug her nails into her palms until her eyes watered. Fury, not sorrow, at all she'd lost churned within. The road became blurry, and she swiped away the tears. "I have a great deal of grief in my heart." She liked the way that sounded and repeated the words in her mind. *I have a great deal of grief in my heart.*

Poignant but not too pitiable. A good phrase to repeat again.

"Anyway, I don't believe Mother is dead," Mary Rose continued, jaw firm. "Those people in her house must have stolen her property by force. I understand the time isn't right to search for her, but someday I will return and find her."

She angled her face away to study the landscape and avoid whatever expression filled Clara's face. The other woman didn't believe her mother lived, but Mary Rose refused to allow those adverse notions to encroach upon her mind. Her capable, resilient mother wasn't the type to die in her middle years. The wagon bumped on a rut and she grabbed the side of the wagon to keep her seat. Mountain peaks soared higher and the road climbed and dipped over the undulating terrain. She fingered the skirt of her dark gray dress, the one she wore to her first husband, Patrick's, funeral. She deemed it sensible to arrive in Wylder clad in widow's weeds. After all, Josiah hadn't died long ago; she couldn't arrive dressed in a cheerful yellow or lavender.

Ahead of them, Emma clutched that ratty piece of black lace she withdrew when she believed no one observed. Mary Rose strove to get a better glimpse of the object, so feminine for their mannish friend. Why was it a secret? And how had she come to travel the wilderness all alone? Black lace was used in mourning. She straightened in her seat. Could it be possible Emma was a widow, too? Though young, some girls married even at thirteen. Perhaps she pined for her true love, lost in some tragic occurrence. The possibility certainly made Emma more likeable in her eyes.

"Marcus built a second house on his land, a finer one with three bedrooms," Clara said, interrupting her thoughts. "He put in real glass windows, not shutters like the old one."

Mary Rose shrugged. Most houses in civilized places had glass windows. "My house in Emporia had glass ones, as did most buildings there."

"I believe the railroad hasn't been in Wylder as long as places farther east. How else might finer goods arrive, especially something as delicate as glass?" Clara's lips curved upward. "Wylder will be as modern as anywhere."

Mary Rose considered sharing her suspicions about Emma's widowhood but decided to keep such an interesting tidbit to herself. Over the past week the constant smile pasted to Clara's face grated at Mary Rose. Life was unfair. Just a few weeks ago, the woman arrived at her doorstep in Emporia, Kansas, bedraggled and fraught. Now look at her, with a horse and wagon and a grin as wide as Gray's broad rump. If it wasn't for Mary Rose, Clara would never have gotten this far.

Instead of gratitude, she had received snippy remarks at every turn. Every conversation led to that Mrs. Elizabeth Cady Stanton or her brother or someone named Minnie. She knew none of those people and so didn't care to talk about them. Worse still, Clara seemed to have found religion, quoting Bible verses at her like a fanatical parrot.

Mary Rose lapsed into silence as she tallied her woes. At least Emma appeared to share her disquiet. The horsewoman rarely smiled. Clad in what appeared to be the same trousers and one of two shirts every day, she at least washed them whenever they camped by a creek or lake. Yesterday afternoon, Emma's temperament grew so surly, Mary Rose held her tongue for fear the slightest contrary word might draw that pistol out. No girl ever attracted a man with such constant frostiness and cross words. The poor thing must expect to develop premature frown lines and further mar her appearance. If Emma expected to remarry, she must try harder.

At the thought of wrinkles, Mary Rose forced a smile to her lips and relaxed her face. Her twenty-sixth birthday was in a month. With care, she could pass for twenty-two, with no one to dispute it.

By noon, they passed a small farm, its fields knee-high with a verdant grain crop, and soon after passed a cattle ranch with dozens of beasts dotting the landscape. Sheets flapped on a laundry line next to a rough-hewn log cabin, a man emerged from its outhouse and waved hello. A marker at a crossroads directed them to veer left for Wylder but failed to indicate how far away the town lay. They rounded the corner.

"I shall ride ahead to see how much farther we

must go," Emma said. She urged Honor into a trot ahead of the wagon.

Mary Rose pressed a hand to her middle, suddenly nervous at what lay ahead in Wylder. Clara didn't even like her, after all. "Are you sure your brother won't mind about me? He will let me stay, at least until I find another place to go, won't he?"

Clara nodded. "You'll see. Marcus is the best of brothers. There aren't enough fine words in all Creation to describe his kindhearted attitude toward his fellow man. I promised you a place to stay until you can make other arrangements. Marcus will honor that promise."

Clara continued to extol her brother, but Mary Rose stopped listening once assured she had a temporary home. If Marcus was as perfect as Clara said, he had to be incredibly boring. Old and sour like his sister.

Clara chuckled at her own words as she belabored something or other about a childhood memory. A farm, kind parents, ducks in a pond.

Mary Rose's own story was much different. Her father impregnated her mother and vanished before a wedding could be forced upon him. Shame and practicality compelled her mother to move two counties over and proclaim herself a widow. People respected widows. More importantly, the law offered leniency, allowing them more freedom than other women to own property and take out a bank loan. In town, her mother donned dark colors and a circlet on her ring finger. She adopted a story whereby her husband had gone to the California gold country to seek their fortune, contracted cholera, and died without ever seeing his baby daughter. Poverty always prowled like a wolf at their door, but never entered, thanks to her mother's wits and determination. *Mother, how can you have died and I not known? Impossible.*

Hoofbeats drummed over earth and Clara reined in the animals. Seconds later, Emma atop Honor appeared at a quick canter. She slowed the horse to a trot as she approached and then wheeled around to a stop next to them. Her jaw was set, and her hands gripped the reins.

"I believe we've arrived," Emma said.

****

Wylder, while not an Emporia, Kansas, was a feast for the eyes compared to the past month's incessant diet of mountains, trees and campfires. A mercantile, dress shop, hotel and theater lined up along the main street. Ladies clad in broad hats and dresses with high bustles strolled along the boardwalks. Most wore calico and simple designs, but several made more of an effort with skirts pleated up in a swag, or an extra layer of ruffles at the back.

Mary Rose studied the men as they passed. All shapes and sizes, some in rugged attire, others properly dressed in vests and jackets. Young, old, tanned, wrinkled, whiskered or clean-shaven. Which of these strangers would be her next husband?

A crack of a whip, the deep voices of men talking, clatter of a passing carriage, and the far whistle of a train. After the quiet of the wilds, the din was dizzying and wonderful. Mary Rose folded her hands on her lap and soaked it in.

Clara steered the wagon to the front of the Wylder Mercantile. "The proprietor surely will know of Marcus as he's lived here ten years. I'll ask for directions to the farm." Mary Rose prepared to hop to the ground, but

Clara stopped her. "You must stay with the wagon. I will be quick."

Disappointment dragged down Mary Rose's mouth for the merest moment before she caught herself. Her perch enabled the townspeople to view her. She took over the reins and lifted her chin to show off the curve of her slender neck to any observers. Unfortunate that their first impression of her was of a woman in a dusty old wagon, hauled by a mule and sway-backed nag. She wanted to be seen as the widow of a respected man of business, not on the level of a hog farmer's family. After they settled at Marcus' farm, she must return to town as soon as possible to establish her good name.

At least Emma declined to accompany them through the center of Wylder, so the woman's peculiar attire wouldn't reflect poorly on her. Such a strange, unsociable creature who preferred the company of horses and a long-eared mule to that of human beings.

Two women strolled by and greeted her with nods. A carriage, every bit as fine as those made in Josiah's factory, rolled past, hauled by two matched black horses. The sight made her satisfied this town had some comforts and worthy acquaintances. She wondered who Josiah's factory belonged to now, if not her. The house and furnishings, a lifetime of savings. Had Josiah's estranged family from the East swept in and seized all? Perhaps she'd been too hasty in her flight. If she'd stayed and brazened out Josiah's death, there may have been another option.

In the window of the mercantile crowded a bolt of sky-blue cloth, tins of peaches, bars of the new Ivory soap, a wheel of cheese, and a selection of lanterns. She ached to go in the store and breathe in the myriad scents. Carts rumbled past, and stocky horses tied to posts snorted and stamped their impatience. The modest hubbub of the small frontier town flowed over Mary Rose. She attempted to picture herself living among this frontier town's simple people, and disappointment flowed through her. Surely, she was destined for greater things, not a place where glass windows were a recent advent.

Clara emerged from the shop, her face aglow with happiness. She climbed onto the wagon seat with fresh energy and took the reins from Mary Rose. "The proprietor knows Marcus well. He lives not more than two miles from here." She heaved a sigh. "Our journey is finally at an end." She snapped the reins and they jolted forward.

Emma waited at the appointed rendezvous, at the far end of the main street. Clara passed along the information she had received, and they traveled together for the final distance. Too soon, they rolled out of town and away from everything of possible interest in this part of the world.

Once away from town limits, open fields dominated the terrain. Excursions to Wylder a long, dusty hike or she would have to beg use of a cart or wagon. A hog farmer was unlikely to own a carriage. She wrinkled her nose. Pigs were such nasty creatures.

Clara half-rose in her seat. "This is it! I see the house, both houses, one small and one large, just as he wrote to me. A barn. And a field planted in hay. There's a milk cow—no, two!—and his work horses as well."

Good heavens, was the woman going to narrate all that was plain to see?

The wagon bumped and Clara lost her footing. She

sat with a thump, then flicked the reins to encourage the animals to quicken their pace. Two black and white cattle dogs raced toward the wagon, barking sharply.

A single figure emerged from the barn and observed their approach along the straight lane from the road. "Bandit! Bella!" the man called. The barking stopped, tails wagged, and the dogs trotted alongside the wagon the rest of the way to the house.

As they neared, the man's features came into focus. Tall, thin as a rail, firm lips. Dark-haired and with a stern face, like Clara's, though his eyes didn't share his sister's worried look.

Clara tossed the reins to Mary Rose and climbed off the wagon. "Marcus! Oh Marcus!" She gathered her skirts and hurried to him.

"Great God, is it Clara?" He drew his sister into his arms and then, gripping her shoulders, thrust her at arm's length. "What are you doing here? I received no letter." His head lifted and his gaze traveled over Mary Rose in the wagon, and Emma with her horses. "Where is Walter?"

Clara hung her head. "Marcus, your sister is now a widow. I have much to tell you."

Mary Rose dropped the reins onto the seat. Time for introductions. Delicately, she lifted her skirts just enough to show her ankles and descended from the wagon. When she raised her head, the man's gaze was upon her.

"Clara has told me so much about her wonderful brother, I feel I already know you," Mary Rose said, as she extended one hand in greeting. He automatically took her hand and his warm skin pressed against hers. As her head barely came to his shoulders, she tilted her chin up to meet his scrutiny. Brown eyes, like Clara's, but made more interesting by swirls of amber, set into his weathered face. "I'm Mary Rose."

His gaze lingered on her lips and then grazed her figure. "Marcus Taylor," he said. "Pleased to meet you." Though too old to be handsome, he had a fine, deep voice.

Mary Rose flashed her dimpled smile and was rewarded with a reddening of his ears. Satisfaction coursed through her at his evident admiration. What a relief to be among the world of men again.

"And over there is Emma," interrupted Clara. She gestured to where Emma remained atop Honor and called out, "Do come meet my brother."

Emma swung down from the saddle and looped the lead rope over the wagon wheel. She halted several yards away. "Hello."

Marcus dipped his head in greeting. "Pleased to meet you," he repeated.

"These are my-my friends," Clara said. "I hope you don't mind I promised they might stay here for a while. Oh, Marcus, I am so very glad to see you after all these years."

He studied Emma for the barest instant and, with an intense gaze, alit again on Mary Rose. The smallest attention, she thought, and this lonely farmer would fall in love with her.

The neat farm, two plump cows in the field surrounded by a handful of sheep and goats, made a pretty picture. This might be the answer to the problem growing inside her womb. She deepened her dimple.

Marcus Taylor will do quite well.

Chapter Nine
Emma

Her intuition screamed: *Get out of Wylder while you can.*

But…the pleasant little town with people who nodded a friendly hello as she traveled a narrow side street lay far and remote from her troubles back East. The animals required respite before they tackled the final rugged leg of their journey to Oregon. Emma's internal voice that advised caution was surely nothing but habit. Fatigue rolled through her. What a relief to be able to let her guard down for a while and rest a bit.

There was plenty of time yet this summer in which to achieve her destination. The horse trader's name burned in her mind—a man known to her father as someone discreet and expert in arranging sales. The trader near Portland would surely be captivated by her pure Thoroughbreds, a sought-after racing breed and rarely seen in the West. Still, six hard weeks of travel remained. A rest was warranted before subjecting the animals—and herself—to the final stage of their journey. There was plenty of time before winter set in.

At least the hog farm lay a fair distance from town. She needn't be on display, forced into conversation and pleasantries, and subjected to questions. The dwelling Marcus offered to her and Mary Rose during their stay lay thirty yards or so from the main house. One bedroom, a sitting room and a kitchen—small, but clean and it provided a rare roof over her head. Mary Rose claimed the bedroom with its narrow bed, an unimportant luxury to Emma. Her bedroll on smooth boards near the sitting room fireplace, no rocks or twigs under her back to interrupt sleep, was a treat. More important, Marcus' farm included a sizeable paddock for the animals with a finely built barn at one side.

She leaned her elbows on the paddock's fence rails after a well-rested night and soaked in the view and morning sun. A blue dragonfly alit on the wood post next to her and insects clicked in the dewy grass. The scent of freshly cut hay from a nearby field sweetened the air, underlaid by the scent of a hog pen hidden from sight behind the barn. Someday, she intended to have a farm such as this. Not with hogs, but horses. If she kept Honor, the stallion might earn stud fees from those who used their instincts and not a piece of paper to assess pedigree.

A crunch of grass from behind caused her shoulders to tense.

Marcus joined her at the fence line. "You're an early riser, as well."

Freshly shaved and clad in tan work pants and a faded blue shirt, he kept his distance, standing several yards away. Clara's brother was soft-spoken, his stilted manner that of a man unused to female company, or any human company at all. She respected that as she felt the same way.

"I enjoy watching the sun rise," she said, then surprised herself by adding, "The best moment of the day in my opinion."

"Those are beauties." He nodded toward Faith and

Honor. Crease lines marked the edges of his eyes, which seemed to her to almost glow as they tracked the horses' movements.

"Yes."

Her stomach clenched while she waited for him to ask the expected questions: Where did she get them? What was the breed? Where was her family? Why had she traveled West alone? Animals didn't ask questions; they lived moment to moment. To them, actions were of consequence, not words.

Instead, he made a satisfied sound in his throat, though whether he approved of the horses or her statement, she didn't know. He stood nearby and with her watched the horses in the large enclosure. Faith, loose of all tethers, galloped to the far end and then circled back with a toss of her head. Honor's ears twitched as she flew past. The old mare, Lucky, remained at Gray's side while he grazed, matching each of his slow steps with one of hers as though still yoked to their harness. Pleasure rippled off the animals, her true friends, and infused her heart with joy.

"Thank you for accompanying my sister," he said after a minute or more had passed. "A dangerous journey for women. Clara told me you kept her well-fed with fish and rabbits."

She shrugged, embarrassed by the compliment and on guard that she'd been the subject of conversation. What else had Clara said?

He jutted his chin toward the main house. "Smoked bacon, eggs and a hash on the table. My sister is preparing a feast. I'll eat after I milk the jerseys. Go and help yourself." Marcus whistled, and the two dogs trotted after him as he strode to the barn.

A kind, steady sort of man, she thought. Clara was fortunate to have such a brother. Her stomach rumbled. With one more glance at her contented animals, she headed to the main house.

****

Mary Rose, clad in navy blue and ivory lace at her throat, a matching ribbon in her hair, leaned toward Marcus at the dining table. "What are your cows' names?"

The woman had accompanied him across the yard as he toted full milking buckets; Marcus appeared to struggle with a reply. "Lily. And Bossie." Pink flushed his neck.

"Such pretty names." Her tone had risen a half-pitch from her usual voice. A sweet perfume scent wafted each time she shifted on her seat. In the kitchen, Clara scrubbed at a pan.

Some women craved the attention of men; Mary Rose certainly was one of those. But the flirting posed no danger here. The woman was the most unlikely of farmer's wives, a situation that called for long days of physical labor. This was a hog farm and, in Emma's opinion, a grislier business didn't exist. Her grandfather had been a butcher, so she had experienced part of the hog business firsthand. Let Mary Rose watch a hog hung and drained of blood, its carcass splayed open, ribs cracked and butchered into chops. The stench of death and innards clinging to hands and clothes. She'd flee as fast as those little fabric slippers she wore today would allow.

Not her business, though. These people were nothing more than a brief interlude in her journey. A few days here, perhaps as much as a week, and then away from Wylder forever.

Mary Rose continued her natter and praise. "Did you build this lovely house yourself?"

"Three years ago," he said. "The first several years, I lived in the smaller cabin, the one you're staying in now." He stopped to blush and then soldiered on. "I saved up and hired help to assist in raising the beams and setting the walls."

Did he not register Mary Rose's assessing gaze? Those sharp eyes that examined every pot hung in the kitchen and grazed over each piece of furniture? And Emma knew the woman was with child. Those quick rushes to the bushes to empty her stomach in the morning, a puffiness around her jawline, the ravenous evening appetite. Emma had seen the signs before. And Mary Rose had no family to offer support.

Ah, was that her ploy? Emma felt sorry for Marcus, so clearly charmed by a pretty face surrounded by blonde curls.

Mary Rose tilted her head toward the kitchen and raised her voice. "Clara, you never shared the many talents your brother possesses. So capable, and able to do practically anything."

Unable to bear witness to the woman's blatant scheming, Emma wandered to the living room space. The room well-lit by two windows put a brilliant blue sky on view. The windows framed a spectacular panorama of lush fields, paddock, and sharp-peaked mountains. Two jersey cows mingled with the horses, heads down to graze. Inside, split wood sat ready to light in the clean fireplace. Summer meant the extra warmth was unnecessary, but Marcus appeared a man prepared for the future. Or lonely, with constant work vital to ease a solitary life. She glanced at him, his gaze still rapt upon Mary Rose, who had launched a monologue about the "best people" of Emporia, Kansas.

Emma bent to pet the two cattle dogs lying on twin dark green cushions near the fireplace. Their tails thumped in pleasure. A long-held knot in her chest loosened. She considered whether softening was prudent, and then added dogs to her list of things she'd have *someday*, on her own farm.

A row of books sat atop the fireplace mantelpiece. They drew Emma forward. She perused the fat spines in delight. Hawthorne, Melville, and an author she had never heard of, Dumas, who bore the intriguing title, *The Three Musketeers*. A small book of poetry, and several books on farming and animal husbandry. Clara's brother read! Her fingers itched to touch the books, especially Melville's *Moby Dick*, an adventure novel she hadn't yet read.

"You are welcome to read any of those while you're here." Marcus stood at the door, his hand on the handle. "If you enjoy books, that is."

"Yes, I do, very much. Thank you."

"I have work to do. Be back at supper." He slapped his leg and the dogs shot to the door.

The three women traded glances, Emma as she stood by the books, Mary Rose at the table, Clara in the kitchen.

"What time is supper?" Mary Rose asked, her gaze fixed on the closed door.

Clara dried her hands on a dish towel, cheeks pink with gladness. A black apron tied at her waist covered a yellow and tan calico dress. All the older woman's anxieties from the early days of their meeting had leached away. Now her eyes sparkled and her words were generous. "I will make baking powder biscuits, like our mother made. Marcus will remember them. And a cherry pie. Did you notice the cherry tree heavy with fruit? Pork chops will be just the thing—"

Mary Rose paled and dashed for the door, her retreating back framed through the window.

"What in heaven's name is wrong with her?" Clara asked.

Emma firmed her lips. *Not my business.* "Pork chops and pie sounds fine. I believe I'll explore the farm, see if Marcus requires help."

Clara tucked her chin down and appeared doubtful. "Help from a girl? I suppose." She brightened. "By all means, enjoy the day." She swiveled away and bustled about the kitchen, a tune at her lips.

With a last glance at the books, Emma sauntered out the door into the sunshine.

****

A day of rest for the horses, she decided. Let them laze in the summer sun. Tomorrow, she would saddle Faith and put her through her paces. The young mare, spirited and quick to gallop, had promise for the racetrack. She might not compete at the new Kentucky Derby, but she might make a fine show at regional tracks.

Two sturdy draft horses led a heavy cart into the far field, where cut hay lay in rows. Marcus walked alongside the horses, one hand on the harness. By the time Emma caught up with them, he was slinging the dry fodder into the cart with a large, wooden pitchfork.

"Hullo!" she called.

He lowered the pitchfork, tines into the ground, and waited until she neared.

"I hoped there was something I could do to help," she said. Her voice faltered at the end. She knew nothing about hay.

A smile quirked his lips. "I only possess one pitchfork and, anyway, haying is heavy work."

She surveyed the field then glanced toward the house. "There must be something I can do to earn my keep. I'm not much use indoors, and I'm stronger than I appear."

Lines furrowed his brow. He picked at a straw on his sleeve and snapped it in half. "You look to know your way around horses. I suppose you've mucked out a stall or two."

Emma smiled. Mucking stalls had to be the worst job in a barn. He wasn't going to coddle her. "Plenty."

He nodded. "Always mucking to do. Pile it on the heap behind the barn but stay clear of the hogs. They can be ornery if riled."

She strode to the barn, happy to be useful. The odor of manure rarely bothered her. Four stalls needed attention—the two used for the draft horses and the others for the milk cows. Her own animals and Clara's mare had stayed in the paddock overnight. They were used to living outdoors, and anyway, summer weather was fine.

A flat shovel hung on a wall beside a neat row of other tools; below stood a wheelbarrow, stained with dry manure. She had cleaned hundreds of stalls in her short life. This was the price she paid to loiter around the prestigious racing stables where her father worked. More than a dozen race horses at any given time graced the stables. Several retired sires commanded sizeable stud fees. Trophies lined the walls. It was not the largest horse farm in West Virginia but had been respected and prominent.

Not anymore. All burned to ash.

She hefted the wheelbarrow with a jerk and rolled it to the manure heap. Beyond, another small structure and about thirty hogs milled about in two pens, the air rife with their snorts and grunts. Fascinated by the huge creatures, she abandoned the wheelbarrow and approached the fence. Two sows, underbellies sagging, ambled to the fence and sniffed at her feet. Recalling Marcus' warning, Emma took a step back. Dust stirred under the hogs' hooves and the unused-to musty-sour stench of swine drove her to the sweeter, familiar manure pile that emanated from horses and cows. She emptied the wheelbarrow and, inside the barn, filled it four times more before her task was complete. Many aspects of Marcus' farm she would incorporate into her own one day, but not hogs.

The heavy hay cart rolled toward the barn, laden with fodder. The draft horses halted at the side of the barn, and Marcus waved her over toward him. "Since you're here, you can help."

"Certainly. What can I do?"

He gestured upward to an open window high in the barn. "Climb into the loft and stand at the window. I'll raise a crate of hay, along with the pitchfork. After you empty it into the loft, send it down again. It'll take several crates but it will save me time and effort in the end."

Glad to help, Emma ascended the ladder to the loft and positioned herself at the window. Marcus loaded hay from the wagon into a large crate, attached it to a rope and pulley from the top edge of the window, and then secured the pitchfork. He hauled on the rope and the crate rose to the window level. Grabbing the edge of the window for balance, she leaned out and swung the crate inside. The sweet aroma of fresh hay swept over her. It smelled of clean air, sunshine and lush fields.

Once emptied into the loft, she sent the crate out the window to be filled again. Hay clung to her sleeves and hair. Below, the dogs circled the horses' massive hooves, but the weighty animals stood steady. Marcus heaved on the ropes and the crate rose to the window. Over and over, they filled and heaved and emptied the crates until no hay remained in the wagon.

"Go on now; you earned a rest," Marcus called. He clucked his tongue and the dogs raced ahead as he led the horses back to the field for another load.

Her arm muscles trembled from the work. She lay back on the pile of hay and stared at the huge wooden beams above. Her back prickled as a memory overwhelmed her. She sat up.

Gilbert, so polite and charming earlier on the evening of his celebratory soiree, had held her down in the straw. In that moment, her thoughts flew to her dress. How shameful to soil his parents' generous gift.

My gown, she had cried.

Well, then, shall we take it off? he asked with a chuckle.

Let me go, Emma said. She wrested an arm free and shoved against his shoulder.

Horses had snorted in their stalls around them. The grooms were well away from the barn. They tended horses in the long drive and chatted lazily with the soiree guests' coachmen. They perhaps shared a flask and traded gossip about their employers. Gilbert's face loomed over hers, a smirk at his lips, and a bead of perspiration at his brow. His heavy breath reeked of his father's expensive whiskey. The rafters spun above her and nausea rose in her throat.

You've teased me all night, he said. *A flirt who encourages a man deserves what she gets.*

She kicked and flailed. He gripped her tighter. They rolled against one wall, thrashing.

The smoke drew his attention first.

What? Surprise filled his expression as he sat back in the straw. The sudden release left her gasping. Flames licked at their feet. The lantern on its side and the fire sprung free of its glass confinement crawled up the side of the stall. As Emma scrambled to her feet, heat filled her face and smoke clogged her throat. How had the fire grown so fast? In a flash, the stables were alight with yellow, orange and red.

Gilbert was tugging at her waist and ripping at her skirts. *Take it off*, he shouted. She fought him, believing in that moment he still sought to overpower her. A horse screamed and she twisted toward the sound. His hands fell away, and she stumbled out of the stall, the heat searing her skin and blinding her, the stench of burned flesh in her nostrils. She tried to scream but the smoke choked her voice. Where was Gilbert?

Bangs and thumps echoed around her as dozens of panicked horses reared and kicked in their stalls. She must set them loose or watch them perish. One, two, three stalls opened, the horses charged past her in a panic, and then a wall of fire pulsed a furnace heat. A wave of dizziness engulfed her, her lungs burned, and her legs gave way.

The shouts of men broke through her consciousness. *She's on fire! Grab her!* In her mind echoed the question: *Where's Gilbert, where's Gilbert, where's Gilbert?*

Then, nothing.

Chapter Ten
Clara

Happiness infused Clara's entire being. Since the reunion with Marcus, it was as though a fiddle had begun playing from deep in her core, enlivening her heart and rendering her feet light and quick. She felt ten years younger—no, twenty—before marriage, turnips and disappointment. At last, life had begun anew.

Dust rag in hand, she closed her eyes before dropping to her knees in the sitting room. *You answered my prayers. I'll never let anyone lead me astray again. I promise. I will be a faithful servant from now until the grave.*

"Goodness." Mary Rose's voice interrupted her.

Clara opened her eyes. The blasted woman stood in the doorway, having entered without knocking, as though she were family and not a guest.

"Are you all right?" Clutching a straw hat with a dark gray ribbon around the band in one hand, Mary Rose tilted her head to one side. "Your face is all twisted."

Clara regained her feet. "Have you never seen a person in prayer?"

"Not in the middle of the floor. I thought you were having a fit."

This was as good a time as any to haul Mary Rose to atonement. Clara glanced at the window to make sure

Julie Howard

neither Marcus nor Emma were near enough to hear. "All these weeks, we haven't spoken about what you did…" She paused. She must not accuse, she must remain penitent, a servant of God. "…what *we* did, to your husband. We are very fortunate to have gotten away without harm."

Heat rose in her face at the memory of Josiah lying on the dining room floor, face purple and gasping like a fish, followed by Mary Rose's revelation she used all the poison at once. Clara's resolution to not be accusatory faded away. "I was surprised—no—astonished by your behavior. I admit my sin, but yours is much graver. I didn't kill anyone, only innocently provided you the means."

Lips thinning, Mary Rose glared. "I was stunned and bewildered at Josiah's grotesque death. I sought your assistance in aiding my older husband to a peaceful passing at some future date. A wife cannot bear to witness a long and lingering infirmity."

Clara's mouth dropped open. "That is a wicked lie. You gave him too large a quantity. If you followed my strict directions, he need not have died in such a terrible manner."

With a shake of her head, Mary Rose turned her face to the window. "I forgive you for prescribing much too strong a remedy. You are not a trained doctor and don't know the difference, I'm sure. Your actions cost me my dear husband and my home. How dare you accuse me of such dreadful intentions?"

Fighting for control, Clara clutched the dust rag tighter; her hands itched to strangle her. Did the woman truly delude herself, or had she always planned to cast blame elsewhere? Regardless, she was a snake to be handled carefully. "I intended to invite you to pray with me and atone. I see you are beyond such remedy."

Mary Rose fiddled with the ribbon on the hat. "I wondered whether you'd like to go into town today."

The change of subject stunned Clara. "In one breath you accuse me of a dreadful sin, and in the next invite me to accompany you to town as though we are bosom friends."

Mary Rose shrugged. "Why shouldn't we be friends, even though we disagree?" She faced Clara. "What difference do past deeds make? The past is over; we cannot change it. We must progress forward the best we can. Use my conduct as a model to follow if you will."

When cows talked and the moon glowed purple. Clara gritted her teeth. "I'm talking about our mortal souls—"

Mary Rose waved a hand in the air. "The church teaches forgiveness is the path to Heaven, does it not? There is no forgiveness without sin. And what of the prodigal son, made more precious to his father by his wayward behavior? You see, I am not totally ignorant of the matter."

What a twisted understanding this woman had of the church. Clara's sensibilities shrank from such evil. She must keep the truth from Marcus, who might never forgive her role—however minor—in dispatching this woman's husband. Mary Rose's version of events damned her even more. Her hands crumpled the dust rag. Perhaps the best course of action was to nudge Mary Rose to secure a new situation, away from this farm, even away from Wylder.

She swallowed back bitterness at being bound to

this murderess. "I will accompany you to town."

A smug smile crawled over Mary Rose's lips. "We could use the small cart I noticed at the side of the barn. The wagon is so very cumbersome and inconvenient."

"I must ask Marcus's permission first," Clara said firmly.

"I shall ask, so you have time to change your dusty clothes. I'm sure he will say yes."

"It is my place to speak to him, not yours." Clara undid her apron. "There's nothing wrong with this dress. It's perfectly suitable for a visit to town." She hung the apron neatly on its kitchen peg and strode outside.

The fields shone under the afternoon sun. In the distance, Marcus slung hay into a wagon. His strong arms swung the pitchfork with ease in a steady motion. A surge of pride soared in her. All this land belonged to him. The barn, the house, the milk cows and horses. He arrived with nothing and built this small Eden from a wilderness. Marcus proved one need not accept the present state of affairs; God provided man with the brains and imagination to shape the world. Woman, too.

Her brother asked just four questions that first evening when they arrived: How did Walter die? Why didn't you write or send a telegram? Why travel by wagon and not by train? Who are these women in your company?

Each answer required careful wording so as not to invite more questions. *An honest man need not choose his words with caution*, her father used to say. Shame over the deceit flushed her cheeks.

She tramped out to the field, each step lifting her spirits. Only Mary Rose prickled at her mood, and the woman would soon be gone—somewhere else, anywhere as long as it wasn't here. Wylder was Clara's new home, a safe haven, although she meant to remarry without delay. Each year closer to forty meant she might never achieve her desire to bear children.

Bumblebees hummed among the wildflowers. The dogs raced toward her and circled her legs, their tails wagging furiously. Marcus, sleeves rolled to his elbows, tossed another forkful of hay into the wagon. Sweat glistened on his neck. He panted with the effort. How was it he never wed? He was a fine catch for any woman. Once she married, her next project must be to find a proper mate for her brother, a godly woman. She owed him that in return for his charity in taking her in.

His eyes lit up at her approach. With a relieved breath, he jabbed the pitchfork into the earth and leaned on the shaft. "Clara. It's good to see you out of the kitchen at last."

She smiled at his gentle joshing. A broad leather hat shaded his brow. How she had missed her brother, who had always been kind to her as a child. "Your work never ends."

"Hard work never harmed a man. Besides, winters are long. I can be idle when the snow comes. What brings you into the field? You aren't going to ask to help with the haying too, like your little friend, Emma?"

Clara laughed and glanced around. "No, but where did she go?"

"I saw her in the barn earlier. She helped load the hay into the loft. Plucky, isn't she?"

She recalled the puckered scars that disfigured Emma's torso and leg and had to wonder what caused the damage to her body. "I suppose that describes her well enough."

One of the dogs broke into a run across the field, the other dog close at its heels. A long-eared hare bounded away in flight. Clara and Marcus watched the chase until the hare vanished into a thick bramble. The dogs sniffed the ground furiously, darting from one end of the bramble to the other.

"I'm glad it escaped," Clara said.

Marcus bestowed a smile on her. "I am fortunate indeed to have my little sister here for a visit."

She faltered at this. A visit? Did he not understand she had nowhere else to go? Of course not. As a doctor's widow, he assumed she had a house, possessions and friends waiting in Missouri. The truth—the part about needing to stay—trembled on her lips. But, no, she must settle in here first. Best if Marcus suggested she stay. Once he understood her situation—with no money, few belongings and nothing to return to in Missouri—an invitation would follow.

"I have a favor to ask," she said instead. "Might I borrow your small cart to go to town? I'd like to see the place and people you described so well in your letters."

"A paltry trade for your fine cooking." He frowned and gave her a stern look. "I am sure you do not mean to go alone. There are rough men in these parts. I am astonished you traveled so far without trouble."

"Mary Rose will accompany me. She is eager to see Wylder."

He gazed toward the houses, as though willing a pretty face surrounded by blonde curls to appear. "Shall I help you hitch the horse?"

Clara straightened her back. "Not necessary. I am a

farmer's daughter after all."

"A fine doctor's wife," he shot back. "Perhaps out of practice."

The mention of Walter faded the smile from her lips.

His eyebrows lowered. "I apologize for my jest. You still mourn, and rightfully so. Walter was a good man and faithful husband." One of the horses stamped its hooves and shook the harness. Marcus laid a hand on its broad back. "I must get back to work."

"I will return in time to cook your supper," she said.

Marcus yanked the pitchfork from the earth and scooped a pile of dry hay. Bits of chaff drifted on the air and insects circled her head. The cattle dogs, having given up on the hare, trotted back toward the wagon with tongues lolling. Marcus had built a fine life for himself in Wylder; she could too.

****

Carts, wagons, and horses filled the streets. Dust stirred up from the activity and coated the inside of Clara's mouth. The men appeared more rugged than in Missouri, with untrimmed beards and weathered skin. These were a different breed of men; hardy adventurers willing to carve a new life out of nothing. Was it possible to find a church-going man of mild temperament to marry and father her children?

A handful of women strolled the boardwalks, a few with parasols shielding them from the sun. Signs on wooden storefronts announced the businesses within and the unpainted buildings proclaimed Wylder a frontier town. Even small Platte City, Missouri, had more modern brick buildings and clapboard houses.

Such details didn't bother her, though. Family—Marcus—came first, followed soon by a new husband and children. This town was Clara's future.

"It is too bad Emma did not join us," Mary Rose said with a loud sigh. "She might have enjoyed a distraction from her sorrow."

Clara stared at her, recalling the rippled scars on Emma's body. "Whatever do you mean? What did she tell you?"

A smug smile settled on Mary Rose's lips. "Never you mind. I do not tell tales. Suffice it to say she has more in common with us than you know."

Heat flared in Clara's neck and face. "I doubt Emma told you anything."

Mary Rose turned her face away. "I have already said too much. Any more would be idle gossip."

The old mare plodded along the main street. The horse had balked at leaving the mule back at the farm, sentimental animal. However, once in harness, she handled the lighter weight of the cart with ease. Mary Rose sat straighter with a silly smile pasted on her lips, one that created a dimple in one cheek.

Clara tilted up her chin. "I shall visit the church first and offer thanks for our safe arrival."

"You didn't pray half as much while we traveled," Mary Rose observed.

Clara bit her lip to prevent a bad-tempered response. Let the sinful woman beside her reap her own damnation. A white-painted building with a cross on top came into view. "There, I see it. You need not come inside. I can find you later."

Clara tied the mare to a post, surprised when Mary Rose trailed after her into the church. The quiet interior instantly soothed any ruffles in her composure. Redemption existed within these walls. No pastor loitered, so she chose a pew toward the back and closed her eyes in penitence. From another pew, Mary Rose's indistinct voice whispered a prayer.

Calm settled on Clara. Why had she stopped attending church in Platte County? Her life there felt as though it occurred years in the past. Poor Walter. She never truly wished him dead and hadn't murdered him as some townspeople believed.

Heavenly Father, have pity on me. I am innocent.

She cracked open an eye. Mary Rose mumbled to herself or, less likely, to God. The woman proved to be no churchgoer, with her peculiar, mixed-up beliefs. If everyone believed as she did that sinning led to Heaven, the world would be in chaos. Clara slid out of the wooden pew and cleared her throat softly. Mary Rose ignored the tactful summons. Too bad the pastor didn't show himself, but she would meet him on Sunday, on Marcus' arm.

Clara hesitated briefly and then went out into the sunshine, the bright light blinding her after the dim interior. Her straw hat provided scant protection from the July afternoon sun, and she tilted her face toward the east side of the street, where the proprietor of the mercantile had been so kind with directions to Marcus' farm. She had been so distracted and anxious to see her brother that she hadn't taken the time to browse the goods or notice other people.

Her good humor restored by the brief stop at church, she glanced back to see if Mary Rose had emerged. There was no sign of her. Wylder was too small a town to lose each other for long, so Clara set off to the mercantile.

A hefty man tipped his hat as she passed. "Good day, ma'am."

She dipped her head in acknowledgment but decided to refrain from speaking to men on the street until she became more familiar with the people and their connections. The West drew many gunslingers, rascals, and outlaws, though Marcus had mentioned no such men in his letters. Better to be safe for now than to risk tarnishing her brother's name.

The musty odor of the mercantile mixed with a profusion of other scents. Leather from boots and belts, bars of soap, sweet molasses, and dust.

Two women stood at the counter as the proprietor tallied their wares. One, petite with auburn hair coiled at her neck, smiled Clara's way. "Hello, you must be new here."

"Yes, I arrived yesterday. I've come to stay at my brother's farm. Perhaps you know him? Marcus Taylor."

The other woman, who appeared to be in her mid-thirties with what appeared to be rouge on her cheeks, lifted her thin eyebrows at his name. "He raises hogs, I believe. Doesn't come to town often."

It didn't hurt to be pleasant, even if the woman painted her face. "I'm Clara Walker."

"I'm Ruby, and this is my friend, Jennie."

Clara noted they didn't offer last names. People appeared much more informal in the West.

The proprietor cleared his throat, a grin on his face. "And I'm Finn Wylder, with work to do, ladies."

Ruby turned to the counter. "I'm terribly sorry." She took money from her small reticule and paid for their purchases.

The women gathered their wrapped packages. "It's very nice meeting you, Miss, uh, Mrs.—" Jennie halted in confusion.

"*Mrs*. Walker," Clara finished with an unexpected touch of pride. Though dead, Walter bequeathed her with the all-important title of Mrs. Regardless of what Mrs. Elizabeth Cady Stanton wrote about equality, society disparaged spinsters. "Although my husband passed recently."

"How dreadful for you," Jennie said. "I'm terribly sorry for your loss."

"Yes," Ruby added. "I hope he didn't suffer."

Clara recalled Walter on the floor of his office, a fly perched on one hand. "His heart. He passed quickly." Josiah's twisted face flashed through her mind. Mary Rose's husband had suffered terribly in his death. She winced at the memory. "God rest his soul."

Both women murmured their condolences and nodded goodbye as they left.

The proprietor wiped his counter with a rag and then tucked it in his apron pocket. "Now, Mrs. Walker. I trust you found your brother's farm with no trouble."

"None at all. Your directions were very easy to follow. Thank you again."

"You are back." He raised both eyebrows and smiled, his face kind and eyes gentle. "Do you need more directions?"

"No, I thank you though. Being new to Wylder, I wanted to see the sights."

He chuckled good-naturedly and gestured toward the store shelves. "Feel free to explore my realm. Let me know if you require anything."

The simple gestures of goodwill from strangers gave Clara hope. These kind faces might one day become as familiar as Minnie Turner's and transform into new lifelong friends.

Although…she frowned…one lady had too much color painted on her face. She glanced toward the door and dismay swept through her. A painted woman! Surely not one of those bawdy persons who shouldn't be out in daylight among good folk. Oh, heaven above, she had conversed with them and shared private matters. Thank goodness, they weren't too familiar with Marcus. But of course her brother did not mix with such women.

Flustered, Clara left the store without bidding the proprietor a good day. The street bustled with activity and noise; horses tied up at a saloon, a stagecoach unloaded passengers at a hotel, the panting huff of an idling train engine. There was still no sign of Mary Rose. After so much time with little company, the sights and sounds of a busy town made her anxious. Perhaps it had been too soon to come into Wylder. She ought to have rested at the farm a week or two before venturing out with nerves fraught from travel and its dangers. Tears of embarrassment prickled. An hour in town and already she had made a misstep. These frontier people and their slackened morals were not like those in Missouri with upright standards.

She ducked into the next doorway and found herself in the empty waiting room of a telegraph office. The clerk in the next room beyond a counter glanced up from his desk and raised a finger to indicate he would be with her in a moment. The click of the telegraph beat a staccato rhythm and the clerk scribbled on a piece of paper, his back hunched over the desk.

A dusty window offered filtered light and the cool, dim milieu calmed her disquiet. She would rest a moment and then locate Mary Rose and insist they return to the farm. The still interior allowed her to gather her composure without the prying stares of strangers.

The only sound the telegraph's tapping and her own somewhat labored breathing, she wandered to a wall papered with various notices. An outdated playbill from the previous year, an advertisement for fine western saddles, along with a flyer for a boarding house and other normal signs of a small town. She scanned the papers absently as her breathing slowed. This was a town like any other; a few rough edges to which she would soon become accustomed.

Her mouth dried up. A piece of paper, half hidden behind a church notice, showed a sketch of a woman. With a glance behind her at the clerk, she lifted the church announcement and choked back a gasp. Thin lips, squinted eyes, dark hair stretched back into a tight bun. A fair approximation of herself, although this woman's face was harder, more wicked, branded by the very Devil.

Wanted the sign read. *For murder.*

In smaller letters underneath, her name printed for all the world to see: Clara Walker, of Platte City, Missouri.

Her knees threatened to buckle. Trembling, she hurried out of the building, the urge to break into a run subdued by instinct. How long had the picture hung on the wall? How many people had studied it and noted her name? A family strolled toward her, four children in tow. Hands fidgeting at her sides, Clara averted her face to the telegraph window at her side and pretended to study the interior.

There was no way to escape the accusation that loomed inside the office for all to see. Weeks on the run and the law had caught up with her; the law had been here before she arrived. Even Wylder, the place where safety felt assured, was poisoned by her past. Fatigue rolled up in her, like an animal too worn out to continue its flight from sharp teeth and claws.

She whirled around and hurried back inside the building. With a quick glance around to make sure the telegraph clerk didn't observe her actions, she slipped the notice off the wall and folded it into a pocket of her skirt. She surveyed the board once more. Where was the poster for Mary Rose, the one truly guilty of a crime against man and God? Resentment hardened her heart against the woman.

If I am doomed to hang, I won't hang alone.

Chapter Eleven
Mary Rose

Mary Rose emerged from the church, her knees sore from kneeling in prayer. Her soul surely must be scrubbed clean after all that time in supplication. *Let me keep this child. Help me find a husband. Take care of my two lost babies. Forgive me for Patrick. Reunite me with my mother.* No wonder older people spent so much time in church; her own list of injuries and heartaches multiplied with the years.

In her mind, she also sang a lullaby to her two babies in Heaven and updated her first deceased husband, Patrick, on her new matrimonial plans. *I only have one true husband and he is you, my love.* In death, her first spouse had improved in stature, kindness, lovemaking, and consideration. He sat among angels and sanctioned her stratagems. An adoring dead husband made a valuable ally. Surely, he watched over her. Someday, she would make a fine widow, able to speak freely of her love for Patrick, but not quite yet. She needed a suitable match; one final advantageous husband to provide a secure future.

Certain God heeded her pleas and cleansed her soul, she stepped into the street. The mare, tied in front of the church, let loose a steaming pile of manure, and Mary Rose hurried away from the stench. Where had Clara gone? Taking demure steps, her head angled down as befitted a woman newly bereft, she considered the town of Wylder. Fair in size but perched at the edge of wilderness with *savages* strolling down the street just as though they owned the place. If she married Marcus—*and she must marry someone*—she'd convince him to sell his farm and go somewhere bigger, more civilized, than this western backwater.

Two men wearing fine bowler hats strolled toward her. In their thirties, perhaps, with well-fitted suit coats. Thank heaven, some suitable prospects existed here. There might be options other than a hog farmer if she worked quickly. One man, dark-haired and dark-eyed, tipped his hat and the other with a neat auburn beard dipped his head in greeting. She bestowed a wide-eyed smile on both. Neither wore a wedding ring, but it was a rare married man who did.

"Excuse me, sirs," she said, thinking swiftly. "Might you know where a lady could find a milliner?" She touched her straw hat with its dark gray ribbon and forced a sad laugh. "My late husband, so kind on his deathbed, insisted I not wear mourning beyond a month of his passing. I shall honor his wishes and order a new bonnet today."

The bearded man now removed his hat. "Good day, ma'am. Please accept my condolences."

"Thank you." She lifted her chin in what she believed to be a brave manner. "I have come to terms with my situation in life, though I carry much grief in my heart." There, that sounded pitch perfect.

"Allow me to introduce myself and my colleague. I am Patrick Lamont and this is James Winestock." He gestured to the dark-haired man at his side.

She gave a start at the name *Patrick*. Was this a

sign from heaven? "I am Mary Rose Culver." To prove she wasn't a common woman who stood with strange men in the street, she cut short the meeting. "I must be off. A milliner's?"

"You must forgive my ignorance of women's goods," Patrick said. "But I believe I've seen ladies' wares in a window on the next street." He gestured in the direction. James nodded his agreement, and the two men gave a slight bow as they said their goodbyes.

Satisfied she had left a good impression and glad this town offered more than farmers and savages, Mary Rose wandered toward the milliner's. The thought of a new bonnet appealed to her need for something to lift her spirits. The bit about Josiah and a brief period of mourning had been clever. This enabled the respectability of widowhood without the drawbacks of somber clothes and solitude.

She touched her waist, reminded of one obstacle yet to be overcome. The reality struck her that with a baby on the way, the hog farmer remained her most expedient option. Longing for the child flooded through her, the ferocity of the emotion a surprise. Of course, she had lost everything—not only her mother, but three husbands and nearly all her worldly possessions. So much time and effort for naught. A child, at least, would belong to her.

She twitched her skirts to one side to avoid a mangy cur who lay in the middle of the boardwalk. Two savages strolled toward her and didn't give way. She backed against the building and clutched the hem of her dress out of their path. They passed with a casual glance. No one around her reacted to their audacity, their attitude that they were the superior persons.

127

The Indian Wars were meant to rid this country of those murderous creatures. Some people believed they could be tamed and schooled to be human, but this was a foolish notion. The two braves wore skins and their dark complexions marked them as 'other'. She tucked her blonde curls more firmly under her hat; hers would be a prized scalp for the Indians to reap. After they ravished her and cut the baby from her belly.

Yes, she must marry quickly. In this wild, uncivilized territory, a man's protection was essential.

****

The window of Lowery's Dress Shoppe featured bolts of cloth and a mannequin wearing a calico dress. While not a milliner's with all the proper expertise, the place might sell a hat or two. She forgave the two men she'd met—young and handsome and with clean fingernails—for not knowing the difference between a hat store and a dressmaker. They were only men, after all. Mary Rose swung open the door and stepped inside.

A short, gray-haired woman stood at a counter, a pencil poised over a ledger. Her neat black bodice had a fine lace trim down the front buttons. "Good day." Her gaze shifted over Mary Rose's navy-blue dress, lingering on the high neckline before assessing the sleeves.

Though it wasn't her best dress, Mary Rose basked in the fact that the cut was modern and in the latest fashion. Necklines rose in the past few years, covering the throat, and the swoop of her bustle was quite daring. The scent of fresh linen and new fabrics gave her relief from the dusty street. A row of fabric bolts sat upright on a rack, ribbons hung on hooks, and a selection of lace lay coiled on a table. Two mirrors perched in corners of the room, angled inward, and reflected her image twice over. The view brought an approving smile to her lips.

"Good day," she responded. "My, this is warm weather, isn't it?"

The woman laid down her pencil. "Typical for July. I take it you are not from these parts."

Mary Rose introduced herself and then added, "I arrived yesterday and am a guest of friends. Perhaps you know Marcus Taylor? He has a farm nearby."

The woman frowned in thought. "You don't mean the hog farmer, who lives in seclusion?"

Seclusion. What an odd way of phrasing the fact Marcus lived alone. The woman had a bitter tongue. "That's the very person." Mary Rose continued in a pleasant tone. "His sister, Clara, and I traveled here together. My husband recently passed away, and I felt the need for a change of scenery."

"I was not aware he had family," the woman murmured before adding, "I am sorry for your loss. My own Henry, bless him, passed away many years ago. I am Mrs. Mildred Lowery."

Mary Rose spotted the only hat in the shop; it drew her like a magnet. She lifted the broad straw hat, with lavender chiffon wrapped around the brim and the ends dropping to tie under the chin. She unpinned her hat and settled the new creation on her head, then twisted one way and then the other to view herself in the two mirrors.

"Tell me, what do you know about Marcus Taylor? Is he well respected? I only ask on my friend's behalf. She has not seen her brother in many years."

Mildred Lowery dropped her gaze. "A single man

has little use for dresses and hats, and so I have not made his acquaintance. I only know what others divulge." She spread her hands wide. "My needs are few; other than church and my shop, I go few places. I have not seen Mr. Taylor in church."

Mary Rose smiled, hoping to encourage whatever gossip this woman had to offer. "I am interested in what people say. As you know, perception is as important as reality. Even more so since reputations are often built on perception."

"Quite so. Quite so, indeed." The dressmaker bobbed her gray head and stepped from behind the counter. "Many do not understand that, but I see you are a wise young woman." She beckoned Mary Rose to a display of silk, the bolts in a rainbow of pastels. "You might like a dress to go with a new hat."

With the new bonnet on her head, Mary Rose fingered a sky-blue silk and let it slip over her fingers. She mustn't spend her small stash too quickly. As a husband, Marcus might not be too generous with money for housekeeping. "I suppose a single man like Marcus Taylor has few needs and little reason to come to town."

"A solitary man, much too alone for his own good," the woman agreed. "Men require the civilizing influence of women." She tapped her head. "Or they lose their way."

"I'm sure you do not suggest he is unbalanced in some manner."

A rap on the window drew her attention. Clara stood outside, beckoning. What strange behavior; why didn't she come inside? Mary Rose turned her back, not ready to leave. The clean shop filled with beautiful goods was so delightful after the hardships of traveling. She wanted to press her face into the soft fabrics and breathe in their fresh scents, unmarred by dusty roads and sweaty beasts.

More urgent raps sounded on the glass. Whatever was wrong with Clara that she banged the window in such an unladylike manner? She let go of the silk, frustrated to have her shopping interrupted.

"I must go. My friend waits for me." Mary Rose sighed and, with regret, took off the pretty bonnet. "That is Clara Walker, Marcus's sister, newly arrived from Missouri." She added in a lighter tone, "Perhaps a bit of oddity runs in the family."

The widow Lowery frowned and stared out the window. "Clara Walker from Missouri," she murmured to herself. Her gaze sharpened and her back straightened. She accepted the bonnet and set it on the display stand. "Good day to you. Come back when your friend is not in such a hurry."

Mary Rose patted her curls and settled her own hat into place. She nodded a goodbye and, with a lingering glance at the bolt of silk, joined Clara on the street. "Good gracious, that was terribly rude. Why didn't you come inside and say hello?" She eyed Clara's drab clothing, a fray at one sleeve cuff. "You could do with a new dress or two."

"I want to return to the farm."

"We just arrived. Another hour won't delay your pie or biscuits. I don't mind helping you with supper."

Clara put a hand to her temple. "I have a headache. Let us get back to the cart. We can return another day."

Mary Rose huffed a breath of impatience. By all rights, with a child in her belly, she should be the one fatigued, not Clara. However, this woman was nearly her sister-in-law and she must remain on civil terms. The moment they completed their nuptials, however, Clara needed to move into the one-bedroom house.

"Of course you must rest," she agreed. "Come, I will take your arm."

Clara gave her a look of gratitude mixed with surprise. Arm in arm, they set off to retrieve the cart left in front of the church. Clara steered her down a side street with a complaint that the dust from horses on the main avenue made her headache even worse.

"The sun and heat are intense in this valley," Mary Rose consoled her as they strolled. "I'll take care of you." She enjoyed the image they must make; the young, dutiful wife assisting her aging sister-in-law. Though once the baby was born, Clara certainly could pitch in to watch the child. The situation suited her very well, as Clara could also cook and clean in exchange for her room and board. Unless, of course, Mary Rose located her mother; in which case, she would live in the smaller house, and Clara live in town.

At the wagon, Mary Rose held out an arm to help Clara climb up into it. They rode in silence back to the farm, and Mary Rose's mind swirled with future plans. She would transform Marcus's solitary existence into a rich family life and convince him to give up the hogs and go into something more genteel, like horses or wheat. Time to grow up, her inner voice said. Take your place in society, have children, and make the best of this man's world. A clever woman ought to be able to foster happiness, or at least contentment, in the worst of situations.

Without the use of arsenic.

Chapter Twelve
Emma

Emma woke with a start, breath high in her throat. The nightmare lingered in her mind, and for a moment she believed the two dead horse thieves hovered over her bedroll, empty eye sockets staring down at her. Behind them, in shadow, Gilbert stood quietly. He, too, blamed her for his death. If she had acquiesced to his advances, the lantern wouldn't have tipped over, the stables and horses unburnt, and most of all, his own life and future spared.

The ghosts evaporated as the dream faded. Never there to begin with, of course. For the rest of her life, the ghosts would be her burden. What alternative did she have? Allow Gilbert to slake his lust without a struggle? Permit the two men to steal her horses and leave her to survive a hundred miles from anywhere? No, she acted as she must.

Emma sat up. Sleep was over for the night. Light snores and mutters emanated from the bedroom where Mary Rose slept. Emma folded her bedroll, set it in the corner of the room, then wandered to the window where a bright moon shone. Memories cavorted in her head like devilish imps.

The days after the fire had been a blur of pain and nightmares. A doctor showed up at her bedside from time to time and spoke to her father, who appeared to have aged twenty years overnight. She drifted in and out of consciousness and occasionally couldn't recall who she was. Foul-smelling poultices were applied to her hip and leg. Someone screamed when they were changed. Was it her? A fever overwhelmed her, then chills shook her body so hard that the bedsprings squeaked. When the pain abated to a level where she was able to speak, she discovered her throat still raw and raspy from the smoke. She croaked out, "Where's Gilbert?"

Her father, in a chair at her bedside, dissolved into tears. "Lost in the blaze. They dug what was left of him out of the ashes. Two dozen fine horses, two more likely will have to be destroyed. Why, Emma?"

She blinked, trying to process Gilbert's death, the horses, and finally her father's question. "Why?" she repeated.

"Why did you lead Gilbert to the barn? Why set the fire? How could a child of mine…?" He choked back the rest of his words.

"I didn't," she whispered, finding that whispering didn't hurt as much. "He tried to rape me. The fire…an accident."

Her father's complexion grayed, his face drawn. "My employer… former employer now… has filed charges against you for murder and arson. When you are well enough, you will stand trial." He stood abruptly, swayed, and then steadied himself against the chair. "After all that Gilbert's family did for us over the years." He staggered out of the room.

Stricken by her father's condemnation, Emma had struggled to rise, but her raw wounds wrenched a hoarse cry to her lips. Fighting the pain, she lifted the bedcover to view the damage to her body. Poultices covered her from hip to toe. She bit her lip and peeled up one edge, releasing a rotten stench and a nearly unbearable agony. But she had seen enough. Blistered, oozing flesh.

An image of Gilbert: Handsome and confident, a dazzling future assured. For a half hour on the dance floor, she had imagined herself in love. The image twisted and his self-assured swagger morphed into smug satisfaction with hands that dug into her shoulders. She recalled her worry about her gown getting dirty. His last panicked words echoed in her ears: "Take it off."

Had his struggle to tear off her burning skirt—to save her—delayed his own rescue? Regardless of his earlier violence, he didn't deserve such a grisly end. One final vision: Gilbert in flames, skin charred, and turning to ash.

She had laid back on the pillow, hollowed of emotion, and wished she was dead.

The memory, only ten months earlier, seemed a lifetime ago. She was no longer the pretty girl in her first new gown, head full of silly dreams, dancing in the arms of the handsome son of a wealthy family. She was no longer the burned invalid, horrified by the sight of her own body. She was an outlaw and an outcast who would allow no man to dictate her future.

The stars faded, and a pink dawn touched the eastern mountains. Birdsong replaced the chirps of crickets. Marcus emerged from the other house and the two dogs raced past him. He stopped at the well midway between the two houses, rolled up his sleeves, and splashed his face with water. Bandit and Bella circled and barked. With long strides, a pail in one hand, he headed to the barn. Milking time.

In the bedroom, Mary Rose snorted and murmured in her sleep. As though aware a man crossed her path, Emma thought wryly. The woman sometimes talked in her sleep, uttering several men's names with a lover's passion or in annoyance. Patrick, Thomas, Josiah. How many lovers were in her past aside from her dead husband? Mary Rose likely didn't know these secrets leaked out at night.

Emma flexed her scarred leg to chase away the stiffness and drifted into a reverie about her future: farm, horses, dogs. But not yet. Another week of respite here, perhaps more, in this remote waystation where hope flickered in her soul for the first time in nearly a year.

****

Five days in Wylder and they had settled into a routine. Clara slaved as though possessed by a dervish; Mary Rose preened and flirted; Marcus worked from sunup to sundown. All three of Emma's human companions exuded an uncomfortable edginess that contrasted with the serene locale.

She fled the tension by immersing herself into working the horses. The animals had gained weight, noticeable even in these few days, and Gray's attitude was positively lordly. The mule reigned the paddock, with an arrogance that defied his inelegant stature. Honor and Faith made way for his movements, allowing the mule first pick of prime grazing spots, and Lucky continued her adoration. Even Emma sensed Gray's unusual magnetism behind those dark, soulful eyes. She allowed him this earned rest, as a grueling journey lay ahead and he needed to carry the bulk of their supplies to spare the horses. The Thoroughbreds were her future, after all.

Faith remained too young to undergo serious training for the racetrack. Most racers in the West Virginia stable started at the racetrack at two years and peaked at three years old. After that, their racing life lasted another two years. Emma drew on previous experiences when she had observed trainers at their work. They accustomed young racers first to saddle and control of the rider, and later to being loaded into and then breaking from a gate. Racing horses also needed to get used to being jostled and bumped by other racers at full gallop. Emma had neither gate nor racetrack, or other horses to gallop alongside to mimic a contest. Still, Faith had promise in spirit, speed, and a love for the gallop. By the time they reached the horse trader, the bay would be of prime age and condition for a seasoned trainer to take to the final stages of instruction.

She took the young horse through her paces down the road in front of the farm. A mile of the dirt stretch lay relatively smooth, and Emma guided Faith away from ruts and bumps that presented any danger. An injury would be disastrous at this stage. Trot, canter, gallop. Faith responded well to a gentle hand.

Any pain Emma experienced from her scars had long since faded to numbness. The early days in the saddle had been torture, but over the months most sensation disappeared. She almost missed the pain as it served as a reminder of her previous self. Now, her heart was as deadened and disfigured as her puckered and ropy wounds. Vanity had dragged her to these depths. Pride over a new ballgown, her own looks, and the attention of a handsome fellow. Well, there was nothing to be vain over now. No man was likely to take a second look at her, especially in these well-worn pants and patched-at-the-elbows shirt. This discouraged any first looks too.

The hayfield lay empty of its crop, and green sprouts sprang from the ground. The harvest done for now, Marcus had loaded a dozen squealing shoats into the cart and hauled them away that morning. He explained they were bound for a silver mining town in Nevada via the railroad from Wylder.

Emma led Faith at a walk to the paddock, intending to switch the saddle to Honor. The big stallion required his own training and exercise, though Emma resolved not to sell him—at least not right away. If he yielded earnings through stud fees, she might never have to part with the handsome creature. She couldn't bear his loss.

Faith dipped her narrow head to the water trough and drank deeply. She lifted her head and snorted water over Emma.

She laughed and swiped the wetness off her face with her sleeve. "Oh, you silly thing, you did that on purpose."

Faith bobbed her head up and down as though in agreement. Unsaddled, the horse picked her way across the paddock, stopping from time to time to snatch a bite of grass. Emma leaned against the gate, not yet ready to ride again. The late morning sun warmed her shoulders. She took off her battered cowboy hat and lifted her face to the sky. Small birds circled and swooped, feasting on insects that rose from the fields. A gopher popped its head out of a hole, surveyed the surroundings and gave her a long stare before disappearing.

In the far distance, the steady echo of an axe against a tree reverberated through the valley. The scents of summer wafted in the air, as though the sun released its own intoxicating aroma. Such peace and beauty here. While the people vexed her, she appreciated this pause in her journey. Soon, they must head West or risk getting caught in an early snowstorm across the Idaho Territory's treacherous passes.

At least the trek forward promised tranquility. Horses were far preferable and more predictable than the two women she had traveled here with. She glanced toward the two houses. Clara, an apron over her skirt, dipped a rag into soapy water and scrubbed an outside window. There was no sign of Mary Rose, who didn't appear interested in being outdoors now that a couch was at her service.

Scarcely friends before, a new hostility seemed to have cropped up between Clara and Mary Rose since their trip to town. Mary Rose overplayed her sweetness toward Clara in front of Marcus, and Clara darted black looks at the blonde coquette behind her back. Marcus remained tongue-tied around Mary Rose, and his obvious interest and growing desire made him restless. Emma didn't want to be around when he, or Clara, discovered the woman was pregnant. Would Marcus be an outraged man thwarted, or a rabbit trapped in a snare?

At Emma's low whistle, Honor and Faith raised their heads from across the paddock. She whistled the same low tone, one she had paired with Faith's name so the horse recognized the sound. Honor dropped his head to the grass while the mare responded to the call.

Satisfaction swelled in Emma at how far the horse had come in their months together.

The young bay had a slight hitch in her step, favoring her front left hoof. With a frown, Emma took a moment to gentle the horse. She spoke softly and matter-of-factly while rubbing its neck. "Did you catch a stone? We'll need to take a peek."

She leaned her shoulder against Faith's warm body, still slightly sweaty from their ride, and raised one hoof. A gray pebble was lodged in the center groove of flesh.

Faith trembled and Emma raised her head. Mary Rose made her way through the gate and entered the paddock. Emma dropped the hoof. A nervous kick could do serious damage.

Mary Rose wrinkled her nose and hitched her hem above the grass. "My goodness, you do enjoy the dirt."

Emma felt her own urge to aim a nervous kick and hid a smile at the idea. She rubbed Faith's neck. "I feel more at home out here, and since outdoors is the source for dirt, I suppose what you say is true."

Mary Rose seemed to absorb the comment and turn it around in her mind to determine if an insult had been made. "I enjoy nature and its beauty."

Emma's lips quirked into a smile. "I believe you enjoy nature at a distance, framed through a window. True nature isn't exactly like the pretty pictures. But I'm glad you are outside, to breathe the fresh air and appreciate the day."

The other woman sighed as her gaze traveled over Emma's dusty pants and dwelled on the missing button on her shirt. She tucked a loose curl under her hat. "I doubt you appreciate the splendor of God's creation the way I do."

Faith stretched out her neck to sniff at Mary Rose, and the woman took a step backward. The horse snorted its displeasure. Sort of how Emma felt.

"You aren't God," Emma said in a matter-of-fact tone, annoyed at the woman's supercilious attitude. She drew a hairpin from her thick single braid, and once more leaned into Faith and lifted the hoof. The stone needed attention before it created an infection. "As far as I can see, you're down here on Earth just as I am."

"I never claimed to be God. I don't need to smell horses and dirt to appreciate beauty." Her chin jutted out. "For instance, Marcus recognizes the effort I put into my dress and my hair."

Emma shrugged and prodded the hairpin under the pebble to pry it free. Amazing how a tiny rock could lame a large creature. She released the hoof and eyed Mary Rose, puzzled at why she was in the paddock if she found it so unpleasant. "He is a man who responds to a woman who offers herself so freely."

Mary Rose's complexion grew pink, and she seized Emma's upper arm. "I know your gambit. You fool no one."

Emma wrested her arm away and Faith gave a nervous grunt. The bay shifted several steps away, flicked its tail, and lowered its head to the grass. "I have no schemes. I haven't been dishonest with you."

"Only because you say little or nothing at all," Mary Rose snapped. "I wonder what lurks in your past. What is it you run from?" Her expression grew sly. "What heartache addles your mind?"

With an angry exhalation, Emma strode away, farther into the paddock. What did the woman want from her?

In seconds, Mary Rose kept pace at her side, her face twisted with anger. "Stop. You will answer me. Or is your only recourse the pistol you sometimes carry?"

Emma whirled on her. "My life is not your concern. I don't judge your behavior."

"Mine? My actions are above reproach."

Emma lifted an eyebrow. "When are you going to tell Marcus you are with child?"

Mary Rose flinched. "Yes, it's true I am blessed with my husband's child. That is not a crime."

"Deceiving an innocent man into marriage isn't a crime either, yet neither is it honest."

Mary Rose's eyes grew flinty. "I knew it. You have designs on him yourself."

Emma gave a disbelieving laugh. "Marcus? Not him, or any man. My aim is to leave here in due course. I have loftier goals than marriage." She took a step forward, but Mary Rose blocked her path.

"Give me your word you won't say anything to him about my condition."

"I will make no such promise, especially one that is coerced. I do not care if you seek a father for your child, but I would not like to see Marcus deceived. He is a simple farmer who provided us with a roof and food out of basic kindness."

"I shall tell him, in good time," Mary Rose said, her voice taking on a pleading tone. "We only just arrived. I am certain a simple farmer, as you call him, does not wish to be privy to a woman's delicate matters."

Emma brushed by, letting her shoulder bump Mary Rose's, annoyed at the woman's attempt to draw her into her schemes. "Tell him soon. I will not lie for you."

This time, Mary Rose didn't follow. Emma felt the woman's stare knifing into her back. She had made an enemy of her housemate. Just as well Emma hadn't shared her own story. She had no doubt Mary Rose would wield it as a weapon.

Chapter Thirteen
Clara

As Clara stirred the thick pork stew on the stove, the aroma of meat, carrots and leeks blended into a savory mix. She tossed in an extra pinch of salt to heighten the flavor, then frowned into the mixture. Had she already added salt? The heat of the stove seared her face and intensified the midday summer rays that blazed through the open kitchen window. The joy of cooking for Marcus had fled. She wanted to lay her head down on the table and weep.

The wanted poster had poisoned Wylder as a safe haven. How could she live here when, on any day, someone might recognize her? *Oh God, why did you convey me here safely if not to shelter me from harm? If not Wylder and with Marcus, then where?*

The poster had been in partial view, with her name covered by the church announcement. At one point, however, her face and name must have been in full view. And were there other posters out there at this very moment, in more shops and offices? She gasped in dismay and nearly dropped the ladle into the stew. She must go back and search every likely building to remove the flyers from sight. Her stomach constricted at the idea of subjecting herself to the scrutiny of townsfolk.

She wrenched open the oven door and, with a

towel protecting her hand, withdrew a pan of perfectly browned rolls. Perspiration dampened her armpits and above her lip. A thin coil of hair escaped its pins and tickled her neck.

Marcus clomped down the stairs. He had gone up ten minutes earlier, after returning from his trip to town with a cartful of pigs. "Smells good, sister."

She noted his fresh shirt and brushed hair. Although he lived alone for so long, he hadn't lost his manners. What if he spotted her image on a wanted poster? The shame would kill her, and him as well.

The front door opened. Clara frowned in consternation as the other two women entered the house. Emma, of course, wore her usual attire, like a little girl playing dress-up in her father's clothes. Behind her, a confection in lavender satin hovered in the doorway. The sleeves of Mary Rose's dress stopped midway between elbows and shoulders, and the neckline grazed the top of her bosom. The waist clung to her middle and an exaggerated bustle with a florid purple bow drew the eye to her nether curves. What was she thinking to reveal her body so brazenly?

As though Mary Rose read her mind, she spoke first. "My dresses require frequent airing and, well, I said to myself, why not wear them in the air?" She tittered and fluffed a ruffle of lace at the bottom of one sleeve.

Emma crossed the room to stand near the bookshelf. "If it's a breath they crave, you should not have poured scent on quite so thick. Your dress will choke to death."

Marcus' gaze darted from Mary Rose to the floor, the ceiling, the walls, before alighting again on her. He, for one, did not appear to object to the dress or its wearer. A prickle of concern crept along Clara's nape. The woman was wholly inappropriate, not to mention dangerous, for Marcus. Why must she flirt with a decent man, who had little defense against a woman's artful ways?

"Pork stew is ready," Clara said, to draw the attention away from Mary Rose. "Take your places at the table and I shall serve."

When Marcus quick-stepped forward to slide a chair back for Mary Rose, Clara's apprehension heightened. His fresh shirt and brushed hair took on new meaning.

Mary Rose batted her eyelashes at Marcus. "I do love pork stew. Your sister is a fine cook and so imaginative."

He glanced down at the cleavage on display and swallowed, his Adam's apple leaping in his throat. "Yes. Yes, she is indeed."

Clara clattered two bowls of stew on the table and her brother took his seat. Emma helped with the rolls and butter crock, while Clara filled two more bowls and sat at Marcus's right. Across from her, Mary Rose lifted a spoon.

"We shall say grace," Clara said firmly, and bowed her head.

"For these thy gifts we offer thanks, amen," Marcus said quickly.

They ate in silence for a couple of minutes, the only sound the clink of spoons against bowls.

Marcus raised his empty bowl and Clara rose with alacrity to refill it. She'd find him a godly woman, a good cook, one able to sew, and be his helpmate through life's challenges. Her brother deserved the best—and soon—so as not to fall victim to a scheming gold-digger. The list of requirements for a wife ran through her mind—none of which described the jezebel he now gazed upon with such intensity.

"I suppose you are accustomed to finer accommodations, and will leave soon," Clara suggested as she regained her seat. "This place is so remote from the rest of the world. We are fortunate to have a train station here. A train can take you easily to a larger city."

Mary Rose set down her spoon and sighed. "Yes, my circumstances have changed now that I am widowed and alone in the world. I shall need to find a position, perhaps as a seamstress or in a laundry. I shan't be choosy for my needs are few—a rented room somewhere for ladies in reduced circumstances."

"Such a lovely dress," Emma interrupted. "And you have so many. I suppose they would fetch a fair amount."

Mary Rose's mouth fell open, for the moment silenced. Clara blinked in surprise at Emma's sharpness of tongue, so unlike her. Had there been a falling out with Mary Rose?

"Sister," sputtered Marcus, "there is no need to put her out of my small house when we have no need for the space." A muscle twitched at the side of his jaw, and he regarded Emma with a frown. "No respectable woman should be forced to sell her clothing to survive."

Clara rocked back in her seat, stung by the reproach. Emma's countenance closed off into a blank mask. Mary Rose stared at the table, the hint of a smile on her lips.

"I do not mean you to evict her against her will," Clara said. "She may not like life on a farm. Mary Rose has unfinished business in Colorado and might wish to settle there permanently."

Mary Rose took a sip of milk and her pink tongue darted out to lick at the corner of her mouth. Her blue eyes widened round with feigned innocence. "I am fortunate to be among friends who care for my wellbeing and allow me this restful visit. I spent my childhood on a farm, and these surroundings remind me of those untroubled days. However, I do not wish to intrude…" Her voice trailed off.

"You must stay as long as you like," said Marcus, his voice firm. "The telegraph lets business happen easily over long distances in these modern days. I'm happy to help in any way I can." That settled, he dug into his second bowl of stew.

"My goodness, well done," Emma murmured, and raised one eyebrow. Mary Rose gave Emma a wary look as though expecting more. A tense silence reigned over the table.

Clara bit her lip and struggled to keep her composure. In one fell swoop, Mary Rose set Marcus against her. How would she ever get rid of the woman?

****

Her life had unraveled and try as she might to stop it, more threads threatened to fray. If only Walter hadn't died. If only she hadn't voiced her desire for a divorce and strained his heart. Why hadn't she been satisfied with her lot in life? Walter was proved right: Mrs. Elizabeth Cady Stanton and her insistence on women's rights upended nature's harmony.

Mary Rose, however, pulsed with menace. If she

murdered one husband, she could easily kill another. After breakfast the next day, with Marcus in the field and Emma attending to her horses, Clara invited Mary Rose to sit with her.

"Thank you, I will," the other woman said, her voice bright as though they were friends. She arranged her sky-blue skirts about her on a chair by the fireplace and glanced around. "This room is so much nicer than the small sitting room in my little place across the yard. I do not say this to complain as I am very grateful for Marcus's generosity."

"He is a good man," Clara said, annoyed to hear her brother's name from Mary Rose's mouth.

"A very good man, who deserves every advantage, as I'm sure you agree."

"Of course, though I'm not sure what you mean by *advantage*."

"A fine life, comfortable, secure, with fortune and family."

Clara sought to direct the conversation away from her brother. "Yes, yes, but let us speak of your future plans. If you require money, I can sell the wagon and mare to help give you a new start somewhere …somewhere else. The horse is old, but still able to work, and the wagon surely worth a fair amount."

Mary Rose stared out the window, a thoughtful expression on her face. "Men have wishes that a sister cannot fulfill."

"I'd like to discuss your plans," Clara said, desperation in her voice. "Cheyenne is nearby, or perhaps you may desire to see San Francisco, which I've heard is quite the place."

"You cannot want your brother to live out his life

without the chance for children."

Clara shook her head firmly. "I will not talk of Marcus with you, not in this manner. We will discuss your leave-taking."

"I confess an affection for him I did not expect."

Clara leaped to her feet. "You and…and…Marcus? I won't have it!"

Unflustered in the face of Clara's distress, Mary Rose continued, "He appears to share that affection, but do not fear. I will not break your brother's heart."

"He will not have you," Clara hissed. "You are a murderess."

"I'd be very careful what lies you choose to spread. It is your word against mine." Mary Rose picked at a loose thread on her skirt and with a quick jerk snapped it off. Her gaze focused on the distant mountains. "I recall your confession the day we met, that you ran from accusations of murdering your own husband. I believed you were distraught and perhaps slightly mad, for I had never heard such a wild story. I let you rest and even invited you to dine. Alas, my own beloved Josiah died within hours of your entering our home, from poisonous herbs you carried. You coerced me to give you our cart and horse, and then kidnapped me." She regarded Clara with a small smile. "I suppose over time I have come to feel compassion for you."

Clara's consternation deepened to dread. Lies dripped so easily from the woman's tongue and tangled with the truth. She sought an answer to provide, but Mary Rose was right; it came down to whoever told the best story. The hair prickled at the back of her neck.

"Truth will out." Her voice shook. Even this sounded like a lie.

Mary Rose stood. With her back straight and chin lifted, she was still a couple of inches shorter than Clara. How could such a small person convey such a threatening presence? "We can be friends or enemies. Friends would be much more pleasant, for both of us." Her skirts rustled of expensive fabric as she swept out the door.

Clara's body trembled with rage and fear. The woman was Satan's spawn. She must warn Marcus, no matter the cost.

****

The opportunity presented itself that evening, with the other two women in their house for the night. She cleaned the dinner dishes, scoured the pans, swept the floors, then climbed the stairs to change the bed linens while Marcus read a book in the front room. She hadn't entered his bedroom before, but surely he wouldn't mind as she was his sister. Though he kept a well-run farm, Marcus was a man and unlikely to bother often with his bedding. In a corner of her mind, curiosity reigned about his private quarters. Did he harbor any keepsakes by his bedside or have any childhood mementos?

With a brief hesitation before she twisted the knob—was this helpful or an intrusion?—Clara ventured inside. She blinked in surprise, expecting a sparse room which bespoke a bachelor. The bed was wider than she might expect for a single man, but that signified little other than a penchant for comfort. A tall bureau and a heavy dark-wood wardrobe fronted with a mirror crowded the walls. Such large furniture indicated an expectation to share this space. She'd been right that he yearned for a wife, but his bachelorhood and age—

151

forty-one this year if she remembered correctly—implied he lacked the ability to find one for himself.

With a glance over her shoulder, she tugged at the wardrobe door with the excuse ready on her lips that she searched for torn clothing to sew. Inside, a single item, a duster coat hung. She faced the bureau, sliding open each drawer. Two drawers filled with shirts and underclothes, one with pants, and the other three drawers empty, as though waiting. Compassion mixed with disquiet, Mary Rose had chanced upon a man eager for a wife. *No. It would not be.*

Shoulders firmed and this resolution fixed in her mind, Clara quickly changed the bedding and went to speak to her brother.

Marcus sat at the dining table, a closed book in front of him. He stared at a flickering candle as though deep in reflection.

He murmured softly, and she leaned forward to hear him say, "Peter, Peter, pumpkin eater, had a wife but couldn't keep her." His stare was unfocused, the flame mirrored in his irises. She waited, but he didn't finish the rhyme.

"Marcus? Are you well?"

He drew a hand down the front of his face. "Sister, it is late. You should be in bed."

"I had chores to do. And I haven't gotten to the sewing yet."

His voice was gruff. "Your eyesight will suffer by the candlelight. Wait until tomorrow."

"Yes, you are right, of course."

He nodded and mumbled something she did not hear. She twisted her hands together, nervous about what she had to say even though he was her beloved brother. Her intentions were wholesome, and she reminded herself the advice she planned to offer was for his benefit. "Shall I warm some milk for you, to help you sleep?"

"Go to bed, Clara."

She seated herself at his elbow and kept her voice gentle. "I know Mary Rose is pretty, but she is not suitable. You must believe me. I've spent many weeks in her company. Wait and allow me to help you find a wife. A good woman, one who will share your burdens and be a proper helpmate."

"As you were to Walter?"

She shrank back. Had Mary Rose already whispered falsehoods in his ear? Had he seen the wanted poster? "I was a good wife to Walter for nineteen years. I did all God calls a wife to do. It was not my fault we were never blessed with children. I didn't—I never—" She stopped, loath to confess what he might not know.

"Women do not understand…" His voice trailed into a murmur and the rest of the sentence garbled.

Indeed, she had not once written to inquire whether he was lonely in this vast, empty land or had courted a sweetheart. Men outnumbered women ten to one in town; competition for a wife would be stiff. Even in Missouri, he'd been awkward and shy among the girls.

"I believe I may understand," she said, recalling his bedroom with furniture built for two. "Place your trust in me and I shall have you married within the year."

"Hetty never understood." His gaze dropped to his hands and now she spied the glass cupped in his palms, and the amber liquid inside. At his side on the floor sat a bottle of whiskey.

153

"Hetty? Who is Hetty?" Her mind flew to the painted woman in the mercantile. Surely not one of *those* women.

"A disobedient wife." He chuckled, a harsh sound. "I learned my lesson though."

The image of her brother she had carried with her through the years shifted. There was much she didn't know about him. "I thought you never married. Are you telling me you once had a wife?"

He took so long in answering, she thought he wouldn't. And then, his gaze shifted toward her, red and bleary: "He put her in a pumpkin shell. And there he kept her, very well."

Goosebumps rose on her arms. If there was once a wife, where had she gone? Her mouth opened and closed, but no words emerged. Her brother, alone in this remote place, had gone mad.

"Go to bed, sister." His mouth turned down, and he splashed more whiskey into the glass.

God in Heaven, I must save him.

Chapter Fourteen
Mary Rose

The crunch and clatter of wheels and clip-clop of a horse drew Mary Rose out the door of the little one-room house the next morning. A two-wheeled Rally cart approached, carrying three women. Visitors!

She darted inside and grabbed her straw hat, the one with a lavender ribbon around the brim. Her visit to town must have prompted a social call. Unless…she squinted to see the ladies better…one of them entertained designs on Marcus.

"Hullo," called out a familiar voice as the light, open-sided cart rolled to a stop. Under a ruffled bonnet appeared the face of Mildred Lowery, the dress shop owner.

Clara emerged from the other house, an apron around her middle and one hand up to shield her eyes from the sun's glare. Figuring Emma must be out with her horses, and Marcus nowhere to be seen, perhaps behind the barn with the pigs, Mary Rose hurried forward to take charge of the guests and establish herself as hostess.

"Mrs. Lowery, what a pleasure," she said. "How kind of you to drop by. And with friends." She smiled up at the other two women, who descended from the back of the cart. Both were slender, youngish and pretty. "I'm afraid Marcus is hard at work, as usual."

The shop owner, now off the cart, dusted off her skirts. "Mrs. Culver and—" she gave a brief nod to Clara, "—Mrs. Walker, may I present Mrs. Laurel Holt, who is a fine seamstress, and Wylder's schoolteacher Vio—"

"Call me Violet," interrupted the other woman, a southern accent drawling her voice as she stepped forward. Large violet eyes made her name apt. "As I'm sure we'll be friends, we can dispense with formalities."

Clara found her tongue. "How kind of you to visit. Please call me Clara. My brother, Marcus, will surely join us shortly."

"We won't stay long," said Mrs. Lowery. "Once I met Mrs. Culver and learned there were two new ladies in town, I had to extend a welcome."

Mary Rose gestured to the door of the big house. "Please come inside out of the sun and have a glass of something cool to drink."

Clara glared her way, clearly envious at how well she handled guests.

Laurel Holt, with caramel brown hair and green eyes, laid a hand on the horse's harness. "I'll walk him to the shade of that tree and join you in a moment."

Her voice rose and fell with a British accent. How peculiar a woman would travel so far to end up in this remote and desolate land. Perhaps there was more to Wylder than first met the eye.

The swish of skirts and chatter filled the air as the ladies entered the house and settled themselves in the front room. Clara filled a pitcher and shuttled back and forth with glasses while Mary Rose kept the three women company.

"We have another companion we met on our

journey west, so there are three new ladies here. You may meet Emma before she departs, but we expect her to leave any day now." Mary Rose lowered her tone. "She is quite young and keeps to herself, but I believe she lost a husband, too. Her grief is so great that she is unable to speak about him. A very tragic situation."

Mrs. Holt leaned forward. "That is terrible. All three of you have suffered."

Mary Rose inclined her head in acknowledgment. "Three of us widows. That is so."

Clara removed her apron and brought over a chair from the dining table to sit on. With such full skirts and a modest-sized room, the hems of their dresses merged at the floor. The house had not been built for entertaining.

"I know how lonely these towns can be for our sex," said Violet. "The men do not mind this type of life, but we women must support one another. I am fortunate my three sisters are here too: Lily, Pansy and Daisy."

"And Thomas is here, too," Laurel added with a smile.

Violet's cheeks grew pink. "Thank goodness for snowstorms. That's when my Thomas and I met. He saved my life."

Mary Rose released a breath, glad Violet appeared to have a beau. The pretty woman with her compelling eyes wouldn't be a contender for Marcus. "I imagine winters can be harsh here."

Mrs. Lowery nodded, her hands folded primly in her lap. "You missed a terrible blizzard a few winters ago. I've never seen the like. It has been known to even snow in August."

"I have never seen a more beautiful place," said Clara in a firm voice. "There is a fine church here and I plan to be very involved."

"Those words do you credit," said Mrs. Lowery, who studied Clara. "I must say your face is very familiar to me. Have you visited your brother before?"

At that, Clara rose so abruptly water sloshed down the front of her dress. "This is the first time I have been in Wylder." She hurried to the kitchen, calling over her shoulder. "I am terribly sorry I have no refreshments to serve. Perhaps Marcus set something by."

"Please don't trouble yourself. We surprised you, and—"

The front door clicked open. Emma stood in the entry. Perspiration dampened her brow and strands of hair loosened from a single dark braid stuck to her neck.

Mary Rose gave the others a meaningful look. "Here is our Emma."

They all regained their feet as Mary Rose introduced them, and Mrs. Lowery approached Emma. "My dear girl, you *are* young. I am terribly sorry for your troubles. Take it from me, the pain fades with time."

A frown drew Emma's eyebrows together. "My troubles?"

"The difficult journey of life," Mary Rose said in a rush. Goodness, couldn't the old biddy keep a confidence for five minutes? "We all suffer."

Emma shifted her attention to Clara, who hovered near the kitchen. "Marcus asked me to let you know he cannot receive visitors. He is in the slaughterhouse and plans to—"

A sharp squeal bit the air. Mary Rose paled and collapsed in a chair. "A dreadful business."

"Not for those of us who enjoy a nice ham at Christmas," said Laurel, her voice gentle. She sat next to Mary Rose and patted her hand. "Perhaps we should return another day. Do feel free to call on any of us at your convenience."

They said their goodbyes. Clara, Mary Rose and Emma stood on the front porch and watched the cart roll back toward town. That single squeal of the pig echoed in Mary's Rose's ears, marking its demise. She clutched her middle and envisioned the tiny being within. However bleak, Wylder was her future; she must be her mother's daughter and secure her prey.

****

Clara fretted the rest of the morning. Mary Rose never saw a woman so unnerved by uninvited guests. For herself, she enjoyed playing hostess, even though one woman a schoolteacher and another a seamstress. Beggars couldn't be choosers in this rustic town. A higher society existed in any place people inhabited and she would take her place among those citizens soon enough.

Throughout the day, however, her resolve wavered whether to pursue Marcus further. He was such a comedown after Josiah, with whom she did not give enough credit when alive. She sought her mother's advice in her mind, but she was as silent as the grave. The grave! Now, why did that terrible thought come to her. Marcus would help her find her mother and bring her here.

The next day, determined to settle her future, Mary Rose arranged her skirts on the tree stump near the hog

159

pen. The nasty creatures snorted and snuffled as they waited for their morning slop. They had previously tipped over the water trough and the muddy sty reeked to high Heaven. She wrinkled her nose in disgust and wished Marcus would hurry to feed these beasts. The spot was out of view from the houses, and Clara and Emma were unlikely to disturb them here.

She must make do with the hog farmer. Anxiety plagued her. Time warred against her. With a baby soon stretching her belly, she must not hanker after a handsome face, or a younger man.

Marcus admired her, but a man like him might court a woman for a year or more before making a declaration. Grady Mills, a bachelor in her hometown, paid calls upon his sweetheart for almost twenty years before he dropped dead one day of apoplexy. His beloved never had the opportunity to be a widow, let alone a wife. Under the best of circumstances, men needed a nudge toward marriage. At the worst—a hard shove.

An added difficulty was Clara, who might whisper a spiteful caution in her brother's ear. Or Emma, who threatened to spill the beans. *Truth will out,* Clara had said.

Mary Rose laid a hand on her still-flat belly. The child remained secure inside her and grew stronger and larger each day. How long did she have before her stomach rounded? Her corset helped constrain her figure but she estimated she only had another two months before her condition announced itself. She must lay out this uneasy truth in an easy manner and employ it to her own advantage.

Already, the baby's face flashed into her mind,

although she struggled to quash those hopes. She mustn't get attached too soon and risk heartache if a miscarriage occurred.

The baby was a delicate topic, but she'd given this a great deal of reflection. She must tell Marcus about the child for two reasons. First, he was unlikely to marry her next week if left to his own timing; the pregnancy would come to light first. Emma or Clara might spill her secret out of spite. She couldn't risk losing a husband because he believed himself trapped into marriage. The second reason was disclosing her pregnancy might be to her advantage. A prideful man such as Marcus had few opportunities in life to be a hero, and to rescue a damsel in distress. She would dangle this opportunity in front of him; it was up to him to recognize its value.

Marcus's heavy boots sounded as he strode through the barn. She sat up straighter as he emerged. He halted upon spying her, a puzzled furrow at his brow. "Whatever are you doing here?"

Mary Rose started to her feet. The performance had begun; she must play her role well. "I-I didn't…I thought to be alone." The rancid stench of pig slop, combined with the odors of manure, made her eyes water. She dabbed at them with a lace handkerchief, one of three Josiah gifted to her on their one-month anniversary. The loss of her house and fine carriage, security, elegant furnishings, and an aged husband certain to die within the decade, contrasted with the present scene. Tears fell faster.

"You are upset." He glanced around and shifted on his feet.

For a moment, Mary Rose feared he would flee. "I

didn't wish you to see my tears. After all you've done to make my stay comfortable, you might believe me ungrateful."

"I could never think ill of you." He gestured toward the hog pen. "I don't like to see you in this setting. Allow me to take you to the house. Clara is there and—"

Mary Rose bent her face into the handkerchief and let more tears fall. "Please, no, Clara cannot see me this way. I'm here to hide from everyone who knows me. I am utterly wretched."

He took off his hat, indecision in his face. "Shall I leave you to your thoughts?"

"Do stay." Goodness, he frightened easily. She must proceed with care. "Now that you are here, I feel much relieved. You are…are—" At a loss for words, she sank to the stump and fumbled with the handkerchief. "You make me feel safe."

Marcus drew nearer. His fingers flexed the brim of his hat. "Nothing will harm you here. I'd like nothing more than to see your troubles disappear. If there is anything I can do…"

She lifted her eyes up to his, knowing her glistening tears heightened their shade of blue. "I feel as though I can talk to you, even though we are unfamiliar to each other. Clara spoke of you so often during our travels. I pictured you, just as you are." She dropped her gaze to her lap. "Tall and handsome and good-hearted. I have the advantage of nearly knowing you, yet I am practically a stranger to you."

He kneeled before her and with trembling fingers took one of her hands. He immediately let go, as though shocked by his own audacity, but she clutched at it with both hands. His neck and ears flushed. "You have my sister's confidence; you must trust me too."

"My womanly emotions are in a swirl." She bit her lip, worried she may have gone too far. But no, this farmer was as naïve as a newborn baby. "I have reason to grieve, but also to be elated. Yet—"

"Yet, you cry in secret." His voice was soft.

He tried to withdraw his hand, but she kept a firm grip on it and spoke in a whisper. "What is to become of me? And my unborn child." She could scarcely breathe. This was the moment when she won or lost the battle.

"You are with child." His head bent very close to hers, nearly touching. His breath was warm on her ear.

"Yes."

She wanted to risk a glance at him, to perceive his mood, but kept her eyes downcast. Her tears flowed in earnest, now from fear of failure rather than the hogs' stench. If the hook didn't set…a small gasp rose in her throat and she fought down a sob. How humiliating to be passed over by this hog farmer.

His fingers squeezed hers. "You are afraid."

"Yes." She dabbed at her tears again with her lace handkerchief. He must make the next step on his own, and it be his idea.

"You are afraid you have no husband or home, but a child is on the way."

She nodded. "You are so understanding, just as Clara said."

He touched her elbow. "Are you able to walk? Let's get you away from the sty and into the fresh air. There is a robin's nest with blue eggs at the edge of the field I can show you… I always think best on my feet."

His thick hand on her elbow, perhaps a little too tight, they strolled to the robin's nest. She allowed herself to stumble once in order that he might save her. An old stump enabled her to climb and view the small blue eggs. From her perch, she glanced down at Marcus, who stared back with an earnest, fervent expression on his face. A nose too pointy, broad forehead, skin darkened by the sun, chapped lips. Once married, she must make it clear her body belonged only to the baby until it was weaned.

As her gaze lingered on him, she sighed at what must be, and his face reddened as he obviously mistook her sigh for passion. "Mary Rose, I-I'd like to give you and your child a home. I mean to say, I will take care of both of you. Give you my name."

Her soul rebelled against this solution. And he acted as though he bestowed a great favor instead of begging for her hand. Mary Rose roused an inner strength. She bent down and placed a chaste kiss on his mouth. He tasted of dirt and bacon.

The deed was done.

****

They strolled arm in arm back to the big house. Past Emma in the paddock, who stared and then trailed in their wake.

Clara met them at the door, fury in her countenance. "What is this? Brother, I must speak to you."

"You must congratulate us," he replied in a steady voice. "We are to be married."

Victory swelled in Mary Rose's breast. Her ploy worked and her immediate future was secure. This house, farm and everything Marcus owned would now also belong to her.

"This is very sudden," Emma said from behind them. "We have only been here eight days."

Marcus gestured to Clara, who blocked the doorway. "Are you going to let me and my future wife inside the house?"

Clara backed away and they entered. "You cannot marry this woman," she said. "I will not allow it."

"Whom I wed is nothing to do with you. You are my sister and soon to return to your fine doctor's home in Missouri. I ask for your congratulations."

Clara pointed a finger at Mary Rose; her breath came fast. "She is a wicked, evil person of the lowest kind. I know things…"

Mary Rose lowered her head, undaunted. "I wondered if you suspected my secret, but I have confessed all to Marcus."

Clara gasped. "You have?"

Mary Rose couldn't help tossing her blonde curls while shooting Emma a triumphant glance. "I am pregnant. I was not certain until these past few days."

"A baby!" Clara's face, a delight to behold, registered a combination of disbelief and envy.

"My congratulations," Emma said, her tone bland.

Mary Rose chaffed a bit, as more fervent acclamations were in order.

"We will marry without delay," Marcus said. "Next week if the pastor is available."

Startled at the speed in which he had embraced the notion of a wife, Mary Rose emitted a small laugh. "My goodness, next week. So soon." He had seized upon the idea with alacrity. Perhaps she ought to have waited until they were better acquainted? Though what was there to know beyond that he was a man with property and a respectable house?

"You are a widow and can't desire the usual wedding to-do," he said in a decisive tone. "Clara and Emma can attend as witnesses."

Clara sputtered. "I-I do not believe she is with child. This is a scheme."

Emma touched Clara's arm. "I recognized the signs in her and have had my suspicions for a while. I believe she is telling the truth."

"She and the truth are strangers," Clara said, eyes blazing.

One of the dogs growled a low warning sound. The other whined softly and padded to the door.

Marcus glared at his sister. "Stop this!"

This wedge between the two was useful, Mary Rose mused. Let them argue and drive Marcus more firmly to her side. She squeezed his arm in appreciation.

Clara's gaze tracked her movement and spoke through thinned lips. "She's dug her claws into you and blinded you of reason."

A vein in Marcus's neck pulsed. He lowered his head as though a bull ready to charge. "Clara, my head aches and you make it worse."

"Your head aches because of the whiskey you drink at night," she responded.

Mary Rose blinked. She did not want to wed a man with a weakness for drink.

A sharp rap on the door halted the exchange. The dogs barked and Marcus shushed them. The fallout from the engagement and pregnancy so consumed their attention, none heard the approach of visitors. He strode to the door and swung it open. A tall man, a large mustache sweeping across his face, filled the doorway.

Marcus frowned as though concerned at his presence. "Good day. This is an unexpected visit." Mary Rose assumed her place at his side to also greet their guest. How fortuitous they could share their news more widely and have their engagement circulate about Wylder this very day.

The man took off his broad hat. Behind him several yards away, another man sat atop a gray dappled gelding with another horse on a lead. The man at the door dipped his head to Mary Rose. "Good afternoon, ma'am. I am Sheriff Branch Wylder. We haven't yet met."

Marcus shook the man's hand in greeting. Mouth suddenly dry, Mary Rose edged back into the shadow of the room. Emma peered out the window toward her horses in the paddock. Clara, pale as a sheet, twisted her hands together and appeared as though she might faint.

"What can I do for you, Sheriff?"

The man glanced over Marcus' shoulder into the room. "I understand Clara Walker is your sister and here on a visit."

His gaze settled on Mary Rose and she lifted her chin. *Truth will out*, she thought.

Marcus frowned. "You are correct, but I must ask what this is about."

"No." The word sprang sharply from behind Mary Rose. Clara stepped forward, her face ashen. "I am Clara Walker. Your business is with me, not my brother."

Marcus's eyebrows knitted together further. "What

is this about, sister?"

"Please, let me speak with the sheriff alone. This is a mistake, and all will be well."

"Mistake or not, you are under arrest for the murder of your husband, Walter Walker," the sheriff said. "I've been asked to hold you in our jail until a representative from Platte City, Missouri can arrive to take you back for trial."

Mary Rose held her breath. Would he utter her name next? Though she felt confident in her story, even an accusation carried a brutal stigma. Her hand pressed against her belly as though to shield her unborn child.

Marcus lowered his chin and glared at the sheriff. "You heard the lady. There's been a mistake." He blocked Clara from exiting the house. "Let me handle this. You women stay inside."

He closed the door behind him as he went out to speak to the lawman. Their deep voices rumbled in the yard. Emma remained frozen at the window, the very picture of someone with a grave secret to hide. Mary Rose tucked that possibility away to ponder later, and shifted her attention to Clara, who had collapsed in a chair with her head in her hands.

"My brother will not believe the worst of me," Clara said. "He will make the sheriff go away."

Mary Rose kneeled next to Clara and lowered her voice. "This may be for the best. Face up to your accusers and brazen it out."

Clara lifted her head. "This is murder they claim, not petty thievery. I have no way to prove I didn't kill Walter."

"And no way for them to prove you did. The foolish man may have eaten the wrong thing, mistaking poisonous herbs for those used for cooking. Say whatever you like, they cannot resurrect a dead man to testify."

"But that is not true. He never touched my herbs. The last I saw him alive was when he ate breakfast."

Mary Rose shook her head and made a tsking sound with her tongue. "That is not the story I would choose to tell."

Clara stood up, a swift motion that nearly knocked Mary Rose on her behind. "I will tell the truth."

"Your truth may get you hanged," she snapped, annoyed to have nearly lost her balance. Rising, she took a deep breath. "Just leave me out of whatever you choose to say. *My* truth guarantees there will be a noose around your neck."

"You are the murderess, not me." Clara gave her a disdainful look and flung open the door.

The men outside ceased speaking while Marcus' sister strode to join them. Mary Rose had tried to help, but some people rushed to meet their fate. She closed the door to the house, soon to be *her* home, her mind swirling with plans for the future. The kitchen window required curtains, perhaps a red checkered pattern ordered in from Kansas City. The Montgomery Ward catalog contained hundreds of possibilities these days, but she desired something better than her neighbors. When her mother arrived to live with them, for her mother *must* be found, life would be in order once more.

Her gaze lifted to the stairs which traveled to bedrooms. No, too soon to think about *that*.

She met Emma's eye. The woman stared at her from the spot she had assumed earlier at the window, an assessing cast to her gaze, so quiet that Mary Rose had forgotten she was in the room.

"Who did you kill?" Emma asked.

Chapter Fifteen
Emma

Emma eyed the petite blonde woman whose cheeks grew pink at the question of murder. Mary Rose had secrets weightier than pregnancy. This must be the uncomfortable bond that tied her and Clara together.

"I heard Clara's comment about you being a murderess," Emma said. "You did not deny it."

"The desperate bray of an accused woman." Mary Rose's tone exuded confidence but her fingers as they clutched at her skirts betrayed her apprehension. "I do not need to defend myself against a ridiculous claim."

Emma glanced out of the window where Clara spoke to the sheriff. As she talked, her hands rose and fell like a wilted leaf, resignation evident in the slump of her shoulders. "I don't think she lied."

"Your suppositions mean nothing. I couldn't help but notice you crept out of the sheriff's sight. Perhaps he knows your name? In connection to a series of petty crimes somewhere?"

The man on the dapple-gray horse dismounted and approached the trio. He led a docile Clara to the extra horse and lifted her up. Marcus watched with hands on his hips as the men climbed astride their own mounts. Glowering, he stomped toward the barn. The dogs trotted after the riders and then circled back, sprinting ahead of their master with eager yips. Emma breathed slowly. She must not get involved. Her future lay west of here.

"Don't you have somewhere else to be?" Mary Rose asked as if reading her thoughts, her voice sharpened like a razor. "To establish those *lofty* plans you spoke of."

"Aren't you worried in the least what happens to Clara? She will be your sister-in-law."

A flicker of something crossed Mary Rose's face. Fear? Defiance? "I know a bit about Clara's past but am sworn to secrecy. I am more of a friend to her than you believe."

Emma huffed in disbelief. Activity drew her attention to the window. Marcus rode one of his big draft horses from the barn, its lumbering steps slow and steady. He waved a sharp gesture toward the dogs and they stopped following. He kicked the horse into a trot. The dogs crouched in the dirt, tongues lolling, their keen attention focused on their master as he proceeded toward Wylder. Despite her trepidation about the sheriff, concern and curiosity over Clara inclined Emma to go with him. She tamped down the dangerous urge.

"If Clara killed her husband, she must have had good reason," she said.

Mary Rose's face lit up. "Exactly. The law does not appreciate the trouble men give women. We are as different as cats and squirrels. There really ought to be separate laws for men and women."

Emma snorted at the woman's sudden earnestness, though she made an interesting point. If both sexes were to be equal under the law, yet unequal in the world, there needed to be a leveling process.

"You argue a good rationale to dispatch a

husband—perhaps even your own?"

Compressing her lips, Mary Rose gave her a cold stare.

"I have business farther west and won't stay here. Though I will delay a bit longer to see if there's anything I can do to help Clara." Emma chewed the inside of her cheek. "After I leave, I believe I will subscribe to the Wylder newspaper to keep in touch with news here. Most papers report on marriages and births. And deaths."

Mary Rose shrugged. "Suit yourself. I can't imagine why you'd find such details interesting about a backwater town."

Emma snorted at the term 'backwater' which she'd never heard before, though the scornful meaning was clear. "I'd be curious to read if anyone I knew died. If so, I might have an opinion to offer."

"Your threats are nonsense." Mary Rose crossed to the kitchen and peered out of the window. Frown lines marked her forehead as she leaned forward to search in both directions. "Where did everybody go?"

Emma flung open the door and tramped to the paddock. The bright sunshine, cheerful bird calls and fresh scents of flourishing fields belied the chaos that churned within her since the sheriff arrived. Had Clara murdered her husband? Mary Rose, also, never denied the accusation, but appeared to defend the right of a wife to kill a husband she deemed evil. Still, Clara had been kind to her and seemed a decent woman.

She sucked in the clean air, perfumed only by pines and grassy fields, until her heart resumed a normal beat. Gray dispensed with his usual aloof nature and plodded to her as though aware she needed a friend. She stroked his fuzzy ears. "Tell me what I should do," she whispered. "We can't stay because early snow will trap us in the mountains. Yet we can't leave and abandon Clara."

The mule half-closed his eyes and swished his short, dusky tail against flies. Across the enclosure, Honor and Faith grazed, their coats shining in the sunlight. Their long legs and graceful bodies defined beauty.

"There is nothing I can do except offer friendship," she explained to Gray. Above, a cluster of wispy clouds glided across the sky. They merged, then broke apart. "I can't go to the jail and risk recognition. We've come too far to be defeated now."

A breeze carried the ripe odor of hogs and, despite her worries, she smiled at the idea of Mary Rose slopping pigs. Marcus' infatuation would wane if his fastidious wife didn't pitch in. Two people could not be more unsuited. Her smile faded. Had Mary Rose killed a husband? Had Clara?

Bella trotted into the paddock, followed by Bandit, and Gray roused from his doze. He plodded toward Lucky, who greeted him with a nibble on his shoulder. The dogs traveled a well-worn path along the fence's edge, their noses aimed to the ground. When they reached the far end, they loped toward a ravine and disappeared down the slope.

With a sigh, Emma headed to the barn for a saddle and tack. The horses needed exercise. Let Marcus handle the sheriff today. Perhaps he'd return with Clara and all would be well.

****

By the time Emma had been able to sit up in bed at

her home in West Virginia, and the pain from the burns subsided into something manageable, her father was dead. A sudden seizure from apoplexy brought on by a beleaguered mind, the coroner proclaimed with a scowl directed at her. One more offense to add to her list of transgressions. The trial, set for the following month, loomed. No one visited to hear her side of the story. Her guilt was a foregone conclusion. The power and wealth of Gilbert's family ensured a conviction. The only question that remained rested on the sentence the judge would hand down.

A neighbor came in to help her change into mourning. She had nothing suitable, and her dead mother's clothes were too short. Her mother had been petite, scarcely five feet tall, married to a man a foot higher. Instead, a search through a trunk unearthed her grandmother's widow's weeds. The hideous, oversized garment hung loosely on her lean frame, but did not rub against her wounds. Emma eyed the diaphanous veil, made of black lace and netting, tempted to wear that as well to hide behind.

At night, out of sight of anyone, she practiced walking. Tears flowed down her cheeks at the pain. Blistered flesh split and seeped through dressings. Anger rose in her at the unfairness of the accusations. The wealthy Parkers' son, Gilbert, tried to rape her during the soiree, fought her, and *she* was to go to jail? Her father took his employers' side without question and then abandoned her to suffer the injustice alone. She steeled herself against the pain and let it fuel her rage. Soon, like the stables, her fury became white hot and through it she forged a plan. She would run. But first she had to walk.

Night after night, she practiced in secret. Twice a day, the neighbor woman delivered meals with an averted gaze. The doctor stopped in once a week with a fresh set of poultices. No one cared to speak with her, the ill-omened girl who burned and killed. Emma let them believe she was incapacitated, but her nighttime forays expanded and soon she hobbled to the kitchen and back. For hours and days, she plotted her escape. She needed money. She needed a horse.

A lawyer, his hair a vivid orange, visited one afternoon while she sat on a bedroom chair.

"Miss Bailey, I will argue your defense," he said, his nose wrinkled against the ripe odor of the room. Dirty linens, discarded poultices, and crusty breakfast dishes cluttered the small space. Her sores had their own sour stink, one that disclosed the extent of her injuries. He withdrew to the doorway. It served her purpose for him to leave the house with tales of the wretched, crippled creature within.

"Thank you," Emma said in a low tone. "My fate is in your hands."

"Er, yes, I will do what I can." His gaze swept the room, the edge of his lip curling. "There are witnesses against you, those who say you exhibited unladylike behavior. Er, shooting guns and the like. Do you have anyone to speak on your behalf?"

"What do guns have to do with my case?"

"Er, goes to character. Meaning, you might have a bad character, er, you are prone to violence."

Emma swallowed the words he poured over her, allowing each aspersion to smolder.

"My neighbor might be willing to speak for me," she said. She clutched her grandmother's veil on her lap, fighting the urge to throw it over her head and disappear under its black folds.

He winced and shuffled his feet. "Already asked the kind lady, and she declined. Er, she's to testify for the other side."

Her mouth dropped open and she nearly started to her feet. The woman had been in her home every day, dressed her, fed her—and sided *against* her? The villain. She hunched her shoulders. "There's no one. I'll take my chances."

"Er, looks bad for you, I have to say." His expression indicated he'd testify against her also if that were feasible. "Trial starts next week. I will have an invalid chair made available, to wheel you into court."

"Leave me alone," she growled at him.

And he did.

****

After Emma exercised the horses, she toted the saddle and tack to the barn. As she prepared to go, a heavy clip-clop alerted her to Marcus' return from town. He dismounted at the wide barn doors and led the large draft horse inside. He started at seeing Emma, and then, his countenance morose, tended to his mount.

After a couple of minutes elapsed without a word, she asked, "What happened at the jail?"

"The sheriff won't listen to good sense. Any half-wit can see Clara is falsely accused. He says the matter isn't up to him. There is a warrant; she must appear in court in Missouri."

"Court…"

The word dredged up the past and Emma's breath stuck in her throat. Once a person stood before a judge, innocence didn't count. It only mattered what witnesses were willing to say. "The sheriff locked her in a jail cell?"

Marcus nodded. "Yup, like putting a puppy in a cage built for a bear. Did they need to surround her with iron bars?" He slammed his hand against the wall and his horse startled and gave a throaty whinny. "He wired Missouri to send out their marshal. Clara will stay behind bars until the man arrives."

"Did you speak with her?"

His shoulders rose and fell with his heavy breaths, face grim and jaw set. "The sheriff sent me away. Said to cool my temper. I said a few things…in anger."

Emma nodded, though she wondered what words had been exchanged. "I'm sure Clara understands and is glad of a brother who cares so much."

He blinked and took a sudden step toward her. "You can go and speak with her. The sheriff will not see you as a threat. Tell her I will visit tomorrow."

Her stomach clenched. *Say no*, she thought. *Tell him no.* "Of course, I will go."

"Take the cart, with the old mare." He swiveled and strode off to hitch up the mare, the matter settled.

Emma's hands clenched and unclenched. This was madness. But how could she refuse? Her horses grazed in his pasture, she slept in his house, ate at his table. People were trouble. As soon as possible, she must leave this place.

She hurried to the house and packed a basket with food to sustain Clara in case jail rations were paltry. If nothing else, at least good fare provided comfort. Mary Rose stood at the window without comment, frown lines in her forehead, and twisted her hands in front of her. Emma ignored her, heart racing.

Within minutes she was outside, up on the cart, and rolling toward Wylder, her stomach in knots. No widow's weeds for disguise, but she wore her hat low to shield her features. Over the months, she'd discovered people paid more attention to her strange attire than her face. Best to be an oddity. Best to be cautious.

Brown wood-frame storefronts lined up neatly, and this time, Emma proceeded straight down the main street. A few curious glances shot her way, but mostly people continued their business. At the jail, she tied up the mare and cart. Was she really going to enter the belly of the beast? She took a deep breath and opened the door.

Lingering scents of dirty bodies, cold stew, and fear assaulted Emma when she entered the jail. Two cells faced the fair-sized room that included the sheriff's desk, papers stacked and strewn atop the surface, and a few chairs across from it. A few wanted posters lined the walls; fortunately, none with her own image. A heavy woven blanket hung from the ceiling to the floor across the bars of one of the cells. As the other cell sat empty, Emma intuited the blanket meant to offer their female prisoner a semblance of privacy.

A young man held a broom and paused at his task.

"I'm here to see Clara Walker," she said, relieved the sheriff wasn't in sight.

Wispy blond hair struggled to be a beard on the gangly fellow. He glanced at the door. "The sheriff is out right now. You'll have to come back."

"I believe she's right there," Emma said, gesturing to the blanket.

"Emma?" Clara's voice, shaky and higher pitched

than usual, confirmed this fact.

"I can't let you talk to her," the young man interrupted, and then lowered his tone nearly to a whisper. "She's charged with *murder*."

Anxiety sharpened her tone. "I think she knows that already. And I'm not here to plot her escape, just to sit with her a bit and offer some companionship."

Indecision plagued his expression. His hands twisted around the broom handle.

Emma softened her tone and lifted the basket she held. "I brought her a cherry tart and some bacon, as well as fresh milk from her brother's cow. You wouldn't deprive her, would you?"

The lad raised his eyebrows. "Let me see."

She opened the basket and once assured no weapons or metal files were secreted inside, he gave a quick nod. "I'll have to lock you in with her. You can have ten minutes, no more. But you have to give me one of those pieces of bacon first."

Without protest, she handed over two slices. If the sheriff returned, the opportunity might be lost, and he might ask her name and other unnerving questions.

Appearing pleased by the bargain, the lad lifted the blanket and unlocked the cell. "Visitor for you," he announced, and waved Emma inside.

The clang of the door shutting behind her, and the heavy click of the lock, made her weak with fear. All this way across country to avoid this very occurrence and she willingly entered a cell. She stiffened her shoulders against panic.

Clara rose from a cot topped with a thin, gray blanket and flat pillow. "Emma!" Her voice choked back a sob.

Emma set the basket on the cot. "Marcus asked me to tell you he will visit tomorrow. I have some food here for you too."

The walls were so close, the cell barely large enough to contain the two of them. A covered bedpan peeked from under the cot, and a barred window, too small for a small woman to squeeze through, set at the top of one wall.

"I never killed Walter," Clara blurted. "I only wanted a divorce. This is my punishment for not attending church, but I've prayed and prayed."

The babble made no sense. The whisk of a broom close outside the cell indicated the young lad listened.

"The sheriff will return soon and…he may make me leave." Emma gestured to the cot. "Let's sit and talk for a few minutes."

Clara sank to the cot. "Mary Rose cannot marry Marcus. She is wicked. I could tell you things…" She bit her lip.

The swish of the broom had ceased. Emma suspected the boy had his ear flat against the blanket.

"Do you need your monthly rags?" Emma asked, and a scuffle of feet crossed the office beyond the blanket. Males were queasy about such topics and it usually sent them scurrying away. She perched next to Clara. "Speak softly. Tell me what Mary Rose has done. I will do my best to warn Marcus."

Clara's throat worked and her gaze shifted to the iron bars and back. "She killed Josiah, her husband," she whispered. "Put poison in his soup."

"She told you this?" Emma couldn't picture Mary Rose confessing anything, and especially not to a crime.

Clara gazed up at the barred window and chewed

the inside of her cheek. "She didn't need to tell me. I was there."

A barrage of questions flew through Emma's mind. She plucked out one. "Why didn't you send for the sheriff then and there?"

"Mary Rose is blessed with a quick tongue and quicker wit. She twists lies and turns them into truth. And I…I am not totally innocent."

"Your own husband?"

Clara shook her head violently. "No, no, never. I may hang for his death, but I am guiltless. Walter died a natural death." Her mouth turned down and the next words were so soft that Emma had to lean closer to hear. "I gave Mary Rose the poison in order to save myself. I hesitated to speak out against her because I share the blame for Josiah's death."

Emma sat back, her head reeling with this unexpected news. No words of comfort entered her mind. And then, before she knew what she was doing, the most unusual declaration tripped off her tongue: "I have killed also."

Chapter Sixteen
Clara

Bewildered by the admission, Clara gaped at the young woman before her. Surely, this wasn't true. "You...killed?" She shook her head in rejection of the idea.

Emma stared at the jail bars, a faraway look in her eyes. "Two men who tried to steal my horses, though that isn't the crime I'm running from." Her voice grew hushed and husky. "I'm accused of another death, a man I knew who attacked me. That one was an accident. Oh," she chuckled without humor, "and arson, too. One more offense."

The information was too much to take in. Clara's head ached. She must be trapped in a nightmare and none of this real.

"I suppose horse theft, too," Emma mused as if to herself, "though they deserved the loss after what they did to my father. His death is on their hands, but rich people don't pay for their crimes, do they?" The young woman shrugged, yet the gesture belied her shaky voice. "Did they believe prison would change anything? Bring back their son? If they wanted me to suffer, I do, for I carry my own prison inside of me, with the knowledge of my actions."

Clara put her hands over her ears. "Stop, stop. None of what you say is true. I'd like to go back and undo everything. Be a good wife. Go to church. Then none of this would have happened."

Emma laid her hands over Clara's and drew them down to her lap. "You can't change the past," she said in a gentle tone. "If only...if only. But what's done is done. I tell you all of this because perhaps Mary Rose is right about one thing: women have it more difficult in this world, so say what it takes to be released. Do not condemn yourself unjustly. None of us is innocent. We've done what we must to survive."

Clara drew back at the mention of Mary Rose. Her upper lip curled. "That witch. Throwing herself at Marcus. She willingly murdered her husband with no provocation I could see. Her actions were not about survival." She stood and paced the cell, agitation roiling her insides. "And you! I never believed such terrible evil lurked in you, too."

She slumped to her knees and pressed her palms together as in prayer. "The Day of Judgment looms for all God's people. You are welcome to join me in prayer. I am in atonement for my own sins."

Emma stepped back. "No, thank you, I will leave now before the sheriff returns. I shall try to speak to Marcus."

Emma's voice faded in the background as Clara focused on her prayer. God tested her faith. What did He require of her? The jail's barred door clanged open and shut. She squeezed her eyes closed and pleaded for deliverance.

****

Clara woke scratching an arm. Dawn light filtered into the cell, illuminating brick walls and unrelenting iron bars. She blinked and stared at the barred window, at first unable to recognize her surroundings. Then she did. The events of the previous day summoned to her mind in a rush. This could not be real.

The crunch of wheels on dirt sounded through the window. A cat mewed. Two men spoke, one of them hawked and spat, and strode past. This early in the morning, little stirred in the town of Wylder. The mid-summer sun dawned early this far north, just hours since it had grown fully dark.

Clara lifted the edge of the cell's privacy blanket to peer into the sheriff's office. They had left her alone in the building. She never felt so abandoned. Not once in her thirty-six years had she slept alone in a house. She used the chamber pot, then attempted to restore order to her hair, finger-combing through the tresses and twisting it into a knot at her nape.

Bug bites riddled one arm and now her ankle itched, too. She kneeled next to the cot and sought understanding—or at least a prayer God heeded. Two Sundays of church missed in her community and this nightmare resulted? Of course, there were all those weeks in travel, but that was different. From what she had witnessed, many people didn't go to church at all and faced no repercussions. There must be a reason for being punished so severely.

As the light grew stronger, she remained on her knees and sorted through the past two months. One of those women—Mrs. Lowery, Laurel Holt, or Violet—must have recognized her face from the wanted poster. Or perhaps the mercantile owner or telegraph clerk or one of the painted ladies she spoke with in town. Her fate could have been sealed by any one of a dozen people she strolled past in Wylder. How had she offended God? A desire for divorce? Voices filtered in through the window, more carts passed by, children laughed, the town awakened. Dismay coursed through her. Josiah's murder must be her fault alone, for Mary Rose hadn't the means with which to kill him.

I swear I will spend the rest of my days in atonement, but please deliver me from the noose.

The front door rattled with a key in the lock and then heavy boots trod on the wooden floor. The blanket lifted and the sheriff stared down at her. "I hope your night wasn't too uncomfortable. I have your breakfast."

Sheriff Wylder unlocked the cell and she rose to her feet. The Wylder family apparently ran this town which carried their name—one owned the mercantile, the other the sheriff. He laid a tray on the cot. The aroma of eggs and toast reminded Clara she hadn't eaten since leaving the farm the previous afternoon; the basket Emma brought remained untouched.

"I'm not guilty of this crime," she said urgently. "The townsfolk of Missouri misunderstand what occurred. Perhaps Walter's heart failed him."

The sheriff's stern face didn't soften. "It's not up to me to judge. By law, I have to hold you here." He stroked his mustache. "You ran away, and that never looks good."

No one believed her, not even this man. She recalled Mary Rose's words, which might divert blame elsewhere. "Or Walter may have seasoned his lunch with a dangerous herb, not a beneficial one."

His eyebrows rose. "Why did you keep dangerous herbs in your kitchen?"

Her lips quivered. Her lies sounded like falsehoods; her tongue not as glib as Mary Rose's.

Clara waved at the tray. "I'm not hungry."

"The Platte City marshal wired he will arrive this afternoon and take you back on the morning train. Best eat and keep your strength up for the journey ahead."

Clara faced away and kneeled again in prayer, gaze lifted to the window. Behind her, the sheriff huffed a breath of impatience. The jail bars clanged and the key twisted, locking her in. Mary Rose belonged here. So did Emma, after her confession. Why were they allowed to go free and not her? Clara squeezed her eyes tight. *I must pray harder.*

Busy townspeople passed the jail as the day progressed. Children ran by, their voices raised in excitement. Women called cautions after them to stay out of the street. The clip-clop of horses, the roll of wagons, and snippets of conversations drifted into her cell. For an hour, on the other side of the blanket, the sheriff and another man chatted about Wylder's growth, the proliferation of barbed wire on rangeland, and the recent hanging of Charles Guiteau, who assassinated President Garfield a year earlier.

The boy from the previous day came in once to give her fresh water and empty her chamber pot. Again, she declined food, but nibbled a cherry tart from the basket Emma had left. As the sun crossed its midpoint in the sky, a familiar and much-loved voice drove her to her feet.

Marcus' face appeared at the cell door and the sheriff unlocked the cell and let him enter. She scrutinized his stern expression, uncertain about what Mary Rose or Emma might have said to him, whether he believed them, or if he was angry at her for shaming him in this manner.

He waited until the sheriff had again locked the door and let the blanket drop back into place. Although the lawman's desk was mere feet away, the blanket offered a modicum of privacy.

"I wanted to apologize for the drinking the other night." He stared at the floor and shook his head. "I am ashamed, especially that you were there and witnessed me in such a state."

Her lips quivered at his humble nature. "You needn't apologize. I am the one in jail, accused—" She gulped down a knot in her throat, unable to say the rest.

"I am surprised you didn't tell me about your troubles," he said softly. "After all, we spoke of Walter."

"I did not mean for this to happen. I didn't want you to know of this false accusation against me."

He stepped forward and took her hands. "False, you say. Clara, are you certain you played no part in his death?"

The question sliced into her. She slipped her hands from his grasp. Anger rose in her at the unfairness of life. How dare he doubt her when he had kept secrets too? "The other night, you said a few things…strange things."

"I suppose I might have. I hope nothing distressed you."

She bit her lip, for his words most definitely had upset her. "You spoke of a wife. One who has gone."

His jaw twitched, and he paced the small cell. "Hetty."

She waited, but he offered no more. "You recited a nursery rhyme. 'Peter, Peter, pumpkin eater.'"

The sweaty scent of horses and rumble of carts

filtered through the small, barred window. Marcus flexed his hands into fists, his gaze drawn inward as though in memory.

"What happened to Hetty, brother? The rhyme, you said, 'Put her in a pumpkin shell and there he kept her very well.' You didn't—you couldn't—"

"Kill her?" He stood over her, glaring, outrage rippling off him. "As you did to Walter?"

She leaned back, afraid. Would he strike her? Where was the sheriff?

"I am not a murderer," he spat. Agony and shame rippled across his face. "I am a man unable to keep his wife. Hetty left me for another man." He sat next to her, and the cot springs groaned under his weight.

Relief surged through her along with guilt at having believed her brother could have committed such a terrible crime. "I am sorry. She did not deserve you."

"Hetty is my one true love but desired more than the farm life. The loss of her eats at my soul and at times drives me to the bottle."

She recognized the opening. "Please let me tell you what I know about Mary Rose."

"She is a widow, young and beautiful, and with child. She's willing to be my wife. That is all I need to know."

"She killed her husband."

He stood. "Bitter woman, you see murderers everywhere. Me, Mary Rose. Who next? Emma, too?"

Her mouth worked for a moment, for Emma had confessed to shooting two men. But there was no need to tell him. Her brother wouldn't believe her, anyway.

She took a shaky breath. "I witnessed Josiah die a terrible death, with poison Mary Rose gave him."

His brows lowered. "You claim knowledge of a murder and yet traveled with her. You served her dinner at my table with nary a word until now. Sister, your accusation rings false. The only consistent topic with you is murder. The devil has his grip on you. I fear for your soul." He banged on the bars and raised his voice. "Sheriff, I am ready to go." His back to Clara, he added, "Mary Rose suffers from the recent loss of a husband and is alone, as I am. If I can help her I will. Now I must send a telegram to Colorado Springs and inquire about her mother."

A sob rose in her throat. The conversation had gone terribly wrong. "Marcus, we may not see each other again. Don't let us part this way."

Keys jangled in the lock and the door swung open. Her brother strode out without a backward glance, and the door clanged shut behind him. The blanket dropped down and blocked her view. She was utterly alone.

****

The marshal arrived on the morning train, an unusually tall man who appeared scarcely old enough to shave. His dark brown hair needed a haircut and his gray shirt was marred with a yellowish stain on one cuff, but he smelled fresh and soapy with a recent bath. From his towering height, he eyed her with curiosity.

Of course, she thought. A female killer is an anomaly. Her trial would likely draw a crowd. As would her hanging.

She allowed him to lead her to the train, handcuffs binding her wrists together. Townsfolk gathered in shop doorways to watch them pass. She recognized that in their eyes she appeared guilty, hair disheveled, skirts wrinkled, led by a giant of a lawman.

The first circus she ever saw rolled into Platte City on a series of railcars eleven years ago. The day the giant tent rose up on the edge of town, a parade of exotic animals and jugglers marched down Main Street. Swarms of townspeople lined the streets and marveled at the elephants, a camel, and one mangy, caged lion whose snarls drew applause. Children screamed with delight when one elephant grabbed its handler with its thick trunk and lifted the man into the air. Clara and Walter attended the circus on its third night. She gazed in awe at the trapeze artists who daringly flew from one bar to another, laughed at the clowns, and cringed in pity and disgust at the sight of the bearded lady.

Today, as the marshal paraded her down the street, she wanted to roar like a trapped beast at the citizens of Wylder: "I'm innocent!" But their avid expressions told her if she did, they would only clap for more. Or turn away.

Her guilt was undeniable—wasn't she in handcuffs? No one believed in her innocence; was it possible they were right and she was wrong? Is this why God averted His face from her? Did He peer down from the heavens and proclaim: Guilty! A bigger plan must be in the works, something she didn't comprehend.

Lack of sleep and food—for she had rejected all her jailhouse meals—her skin scratched raw from the bug bites, distress, and fear clouded her mind.

"Guilty," she muttered. "I am guilty."

The young marshal yanked her forward. "That's why I'm here. To take you back so justice can be served."

The mournful cry of the train whistle cut through

the air. They waited on the station platform as the huge metal beast belched smoke and chugged to a stop. Passengers made a wide berth around her, staring a silent accusation. The good people of Wylder must be kept safe from desperados such as she. Her gaze lifted and searched, a final spark of hope flickering in her heart before it turned to ash.

Marcus had not come to say goodbye.

Chapter Seventeen
Mary Rose

Mary Rose wrapped the apron around her midsection and set about making dinner. In the distance, a train whistle announced its departure from Wylder. If there was any justice in the world, Clara would not hang for her husband's murder. A woman should *not* be hanged for killing a husband. Any sensible judge should understand that.

Though she didn't want Clara gone forever, a temporary separation of Marcus from his sister suited her during this delicate time between the proposal and the wedding. She pressed her fingers against her eyelids. *Think! Were there any other options at all?*

Her eyes watered and tears threatened to spill out. She swiped them away with the back of her hand. If her mother taught her nothing else, it was to survive. Hot tears spilled out now at the memory of her mother, wetting her cheeks. How much must she endure?

She glanced at the window. In the far field where a small crop of corn rose shoulder high, Marcus bent to work with a hoe in his hands. Over and over, he chopped at the dirt. Even from this distance she observed the dark sweat stain on the back of his shirt. Why did he have to get so filthy? Why couldn't he hire a man or two?

He had returned from the jail the previous day in a

foul mood, chin down and mood dark.

"She'll hang," he said abruptly when Mary Rose ran out to greet him on his arrival.

"Surely not," she had said, holding a hand to her throat.

He didn't offer comfort as any other man might have done at her distress. "I've lost half a day's work." His expression shifted, an unfamiliar glint behind his eyes. A muscle in his jaw twitched and with a terse "I will speak to you later," he strode away.

His manner then had been different toward her, less admiring and tender. What had Clara disclosed? Why didn't he accuse her straight out so she could defend herself? Doubts troubled her the rest of that day. She washed her clothes and bed linens and hung them out to dry. The hot summer sun made quick work of the laundry, which was fortunate since her delicates were on display. She tugged them off the line and dropped them into a basket. A foul odor emanated from her freshly washed clothes. The breeze had shifted and the scent of pigs clung to her laundry.

In the distance, Emma had crossed a field to where Marcus kneeled in the soil, head lowered as if in prayer. Mary Rose recalled how her breath quickened with the fear of losing everything once more. She had grabbed a bedsheet on the line to steady herself. At the memory, her hands gripped her apron, eyes glazed with remembering.

Marcus had risen to his feet and he and Emma stood, their backs to her. Were they plotting together to send her to jail with Clara? If Clara was doomed to the noose, then she might follow. Her throat closed as though the rope already knotted and tightened. Panic nearly overtook her as a vision of herself racing away on horseback flashed through her mind.

Even now, at the kitchen window a day later, her heart beat faster in memory, her mouth dry as she recalled her fear.

Minutes had passed and still they conversed. Suddenly, Emma broke away and headed to the paddock, without a glance in her direction. Perhaps they spoke only of horses and farms? Marcus remained standing, still as a stone, his back rigid. No, Emma must have accused her. Mary Rose's heart fluttered faster. Marcus swung around, his face stern, and Mary Rose almost fainted.

Please God, if you give me nothing else, rescue me from a gruesome end. I will mend my ways, forever and ever. Remember, I am with child and have mercy.

Marcus approached with lengthy strides and any remaining moisture in her mouth dried up. His long legs appeared spindly and awkward. The idea of living under one roof with him for the rest of her days—if indeed God granted her plea—made her cringe. He swept up her hands in his. Dirt clung to his knuckles and under his fingernails. Hard calluses scraped against her skin. She stared at his hands, unable to meet a gaze that must be cold with wrath and condemnation.

"Forgive me, Mary Rose. I should not withhold this information from you a moment longer. I could not bear to hurt you after all your suffering."

She glanced up in surprise. His manner was far from accusatory; perhaps Clara and Emma hadn't blabbed. She forced a neutral tone, though her legs trembled. "Tell me what troubles you, dear Marcus."

"I sent the telegram you requested about your

mother to the sheriff in Colorado Springs. A reply came immediately. I am afraid he confirmed her death. Scarlet fever."

A mixture of relief and anguish coursed through her. "Scarlet fever! That's a child's illness."

He drew her against his rigid chest with what he must believe to be a comforting embrace. "Does it matter how she died? You must take comfort in knowing she is in Heaven." He stepped back and frowned down at her. "She was a godly woman?"

Mary Rose had nodded, numbed by the news, though her mother never attended church. What difference did it make if she was in Heaven when she was dead *now*? "She can't be gone. She can't have left me alone."

Marcus drew her to him again, this time in a confining squeeze. "You are not alone and will never be again. I will take care of you. There is plenty of work to be done on the farm. I've always found labor to be a great healer."

Mother, dead! Before her, nothing but work. But no mention of Josiah and poison, thanks to her bargain with God.

Her heart wrenched in her chest. Marriage to this pig man promised to be a fate every bit as terrible as the one Clara suffered. She wiggled loose. "Yes, but we must delay the wedding. I shall send a marker to my mother's grave and...and...pray for her soul." She stared at him, willing him to return to the fields and stop touching her.

He gripped her wrists now, handcuffing them in his strong fingers. This was a sensation she didn't care for at all. "It is not seemly for you to live on the farm with me while we are not married. I will not shame my future wife that way."

She tugged away, annoyed at his insistence, wanting to be free to think about her mother. To cry and keen in private. To assess any loopholes in her promise to God. "Oh, blast the gossips! Let us do what as we please. A month will not matter."

"I know you are upset and this is what makes you use profane words. Your shame becomes my shame. We will marry quickly, so the world acknowledges your child as my child. Just think how it would appear if we lived here together unmarried for a month and then you had an early birth." He paused and another— undefinable—note colored his tone. "You will marry me, and I will shelter you and your child as I promised."

The rest of the conversation the previous day became murky in her memory as she stood at the kitchen window. With Clara gone, Marcus insisted they marry by week's end to avoid any nasty gossip. As if the gossips weren't already busy enough with his sister's arrest.

Her collar damp with tears, she sobbed freely now, letting the drops roll off her chin into the sink. She was trapped in a web of her own making. No mother, no friends, alone in the world. Mary Rose touched her belly. *Except for you, little one*. Her tears dried up. A little girl to raise, cosset and adore, one with blonde curls like her own. A pint-sized beauty to grow up and capture the heart of a wealthy man and achieve everything Mary Rose had not. Motherhood could be her solace. Outside, the hoe rose and fell in a steady rhythm.

That tone, at the end, when he insisted they marry soon. Something in it conveyed a threat. *He suspected.*

****

A day passed. And then another. No word arrived from Missouri about Clara's fate. Emma glowered at Mary Rose each time she came near, and Mary Rose avoided any chance of their being alone together. Meal conversations, stiff and enlivened only by her strongest efforts, received little contribution from Marcus or Emma. In the evenings, Mary Rose closeted herself in the single bedroom before Emma entered the little house. On the third day after the marshal took Clara away, Emma remained in the big house after breakfast. She gathered the dishes from the table. "I will help clean up."

Mary Rose gave a nervous laugh and spluttered. "Oh my, no. You must go be with your horses."

Saying nothing, Emma carried dishes to the large farmhouse sink. As he had done the last couple of days, Marcus headed to town to wire Platte City for news of Clara.

The moment he left the house, Emma took her dripping hands out of the sudsy water. The water puddled on the floor at her boots. "You have caught me up in your schemes. I'd have been far away from here by now if not for you. Marcus asked me to stay until the two of you were wed, to keep gossip away. Marry him so I may leave."

All Mary Rose's earlier confidence failed her confronted with this younger woman who appeared to need no one and nothing. "What did you say to him about me? Tell me, I must know."

"I made a promise to Clara to warn her brother

about you." Emma's lip curled. "She told me everything."

Mary Rose dumped the cutlery she carried into the wash basin with a splash. Clara! Even in jail, she was a thorn in her side. "I'm sure she told you her version of events."

Emma shrugged and wiped her hands on her trousers, leaving a dark, wet mark. "I believe her since the confession damns her. You are fortunate in that Marcus wishes for a wife. He can't conceive a pretty face may hide a threat."

Mary Rose swallowed, panic causing words to rush out. "Take me with you when you leave."

Emma's eyes widened. "You are to marry Marcus. You gave him your promise."

Fear nibbled at the edges of Mary Rose's composure. "I may have been too hasty. I have a little money and a silver service I'm sure is worth something. If you are going to San Francisco, perhaps I'd have better luck there."

"That is not my destination. In any case, I prefer to travel alone. May I offer you some advice?"

Mary Rose sniffed, provoked from her anxiety by the ill-mannered refusal. "You, a girl in men's pants? Give me counsel? Your own head is muddled. I doubt you have anything wise to say."

"Marry Marcus and be grateful. You could not do better."

"I could crook my little finger and marry who I like." Mary Rose wished this was true. Handsome, younger men abounded in Wylder. But which of them wished for a pregnant, thrice-married bride?

Emma shook her head. "Let us be honest with each

other. At least on this subject. You have killed a husband, and taken lovers outside marriage, for you talk in your sleep."

Outrage surged. "I have *never* committed adultery."

"Who is Patrick?" Emma's voice sharpened. "And Thomas?"

Mary Rose's breath hitched in her throat. No one had ever accused her of talking in her sleep. All those weeks of travel, sleeping in the wagon next to Clara. It wasn't politic to utter other men's names in the middle of the night, especially those not currently married to. Chin down, she defended her honor. "I had many beaus before I was married."

Emma leaned against the wash tub and her shoulders sagged. "I'm tired of strife and bitter words. I want to leave. You sought Marcus' attentions and he proposed. He will hear nothing bad about you despite his own sister's claims. Marry him, be true, and find happiness."

Tears pooled in Mary Rose's eyes. Emma was right. While this farmer had few physical advantages, he believed in her innocence and offered her a home.

With stiff shoulders, they stood side by side and finished the dishes. Once done, Emma crossed to the next room and snatched a book from the shelf. She plopped onto a chair, her jerky movements betraying her annoyance. Mary Rose perched on a chair across from this strange creature, prickly in nature, who didn't seem to care about her appearance or what anyone thought about her. The woman planned to ride off into the mountains, utterly alone, with no indication of fear or need for the protection of a man. The very idea of being alone like that sent shivers down Mary Rose's spine. Emma was like a wild animal—nothing as ferocious as a lion, but more of a badger or a porcupine.

Emma glanced up from the pages and raised an eyebrow. Mary Rose bit her lip and gestured to the book. "What do you find so interesting in storybooks? I never had the patience to sit and pore through sentence after sentence." She touched the side of her forehead and gave a small laugh. "The words dance around and make my head ache."

Emma sat back with a reflective expression. She laid a hand on the page. "The words take me to places I have never been or am likely to go. They teach about grand ideas and circumstances in which other people are forced to live. When I'm down, stories have the power to make me laugh."

"My mother used to tell me stories when I was little. But I do not think Mother wanted me to waste my time with a book on my lap. Though"—a memory caused a smile to flit at her mouth—"I remember how nice it was at night to have her sit on my bed and stroke my hair. She told me about Cinderella and the magical bird that threw down a golden dress for her to wear to the dance, and then the bird pecked out the eyes of her terrible stepsisters." Mary Rose lifted her chin. "Mother said if I was beautiful, I would marry a rich man and be happy like Cinderella. And any enemies I might have would suffer." Her voice trailed off as she recalled her lingering childhood belief in a fairy-tale ending.

Emma shrugged and glanced down at the book. "I always supposed that tale was about being kind and honest."

Mary Rose's forehead wrinkled. She didn't recall

that part of the story.

Emma leaned forward. "Some stories are not meant to be literal. For instance, reading about courageous people gives me courage. I think, if they can do it, so can I."

"You mean you playact and pretend you are a character?" Emma shook her head, but the idea of taking on another's attributes captured Mary Rose's imagination. "Do you suppose we can trick ourselves into believing things that aren't true?"

"I think that happens every day, dozens of times a day for some people. The poet John Milton writes our minds can create a heaven of hell or a hell of heaven."

Mary Rose gazed out the window where formidably high, green mountains loomed in the distance, confining the valley like the bars of a jail cell. Perhaps she could pretend Marcus was as handsome as a prince, or even—could this be possible?—an incarnate of her true love, Patrick. Such a trick of the mind would indeed make a heaven of this impending hell. She returned her attention to Emma and her tone grew fierce. "How does one go about convincing oneself of a fiction?"

"You have to want to believe. That's the first step."

Her jaw set, Mary Rose regained her feet. *Patrick, I can make you live again. This baby inside me can be ours.*

Hope swelled in her chest. She glanced out the window again. Marcus appeared in the distance, his horse in a lather from a hard ride to and from town. Her first husband had been slighter in build, younger, with a livelier personality, and so very handsome. Maybe there was some minute element of Marcus similar to Patrick;

then she might focus on that and build her fiction. "My husband-to-be is back from town. I will see if there's news—and take him something cold to drink."

Emma regarded her with a curious look and then bowed her head to the pages. Mary Rose crossed to the kitchen and poured a large glass of cool water from a pitcher. She emerged from the house into harsh daylight, the glare from the midday sun nearly unbearable. No fiction could stop the summer heat.

Marcus had put away the horse and wielded a hoe by the time she reached him. He halted halfway to the field to watch her approach.

"You have thirsty work ahead," she said, handing him the glass.

His gaze burned into her and she felt devoured under the steady stare. He gulped the water and his Adam's apple bobbed with each swallow until the glass was emptied. Had Patrick ever observed her so intently?

"Thank you. You are as kind as you are beautiful."

"Any word about Clara?" she asked to be polite.

He shook his head, lips thinned. "You've been a good friend to my sister. Better than she deserves."

The praise warmed her, and she rewarded him with a view of her dimple. How little thanks she received from Clara. "I aided her in every way possible, though it never seemed enough."

A streak of dirt smudged his brow, but a memory struck her of Patrick, who also had been a farmer. One evening, he entered their home with dirt above his upper lip, giving him the appearance of a mustache. How she had laughed and wiped the grime away. Before she thought twice, she stretched a hand up and brushed Marcus' forehead. "Heavens, but you have half the farm on your face," she scolded lightly, as she might have done with Patrick.

Marcus chuckled, his eyes lit in happiness again, and caught up her hand. "You are marrying a farmer, so you'll need to be prepared for this and more."

She stared at his dirt-crusted boots. This pretense would take every ounce of strength she had. It helped if she didn't look directly at him. "I am ready to marry you, tomorrow if possible."

He gulped and sputtered. "I will go at once to speak with the pastor. A generous contribution should persuade him to make time." He squeezed her fingers. "Mary Rose, I will strive every day to be worthy of your love. You will want for nothing. You and...our child."

"Dear, do not tire yourself out by another hard ride so soon," she said. Patrick's image danced before her. How excited she had been to marry him. She nearly ran to the altar. "This afternoon will be soon enough."

He squeezed her hand tighter, and she recalled Patrick's passionate embraces. "Tomorrow, we will shift your belongings into the main house. And all I have will be yours."

Sweet words. Even Patrick had never made such promises, although to be fair, her first husband had very little. A twinge in her belly felt slightly of desire. She marveled at the success of Mr. John Milton's advice in his poetry. How did Emma articulate it? If you don't like reality, make it up—or something like that. Whoever knew anything useful came out of books?

****

Late that afternoon, while Emma and Mary Rose

shared in the dinner preparations, Marcus returned from town, speaking fast with excitement. "The pastor can marry us tomorrow. Cost me two smoked hams."

Mary Rose lifted her chin, trying not to think about a hog carcass mixed up with her nuptials. The trade seemed slightly crude, and she hoped the hams didn't change hands in her presence. "Tomorrow will be a fine day for a wedding. I will wear my yellow dress and carry a posy of wildflowers." She took a deep breath. One further ruse had occurred to her. "I have one request, Marcus dear. I'd like my middle name to be my legal name."

"Your name suits you so well," he said, a frown of puzzlement on his forehead. "I suppose it can't do any harm. What is your middle name?"

"Bathsheba."

Across the room, Emma stifled a guffaw.

She glared at Emma. "My new name is nothing to laugh at. It's from the Bible." It would also erase all traces of Mary Rose Culver, in case the Emporia sheriff ever nosed around these parts. She gripped Marcus' hand. "She was the wife of a king."

He squeezed her hand and gazed at her approvingly. "Bathsheba. If I recall, she was a beautiful woman the king couldn't resist."

"Wasn't she a widow as well?" Emma asked. "Her first husband was killed as I recall."

"Yes, well enough of Bible stories," Mary Rose interrupted. "I only want to mark the start of my new life here with Marcus."

"Then Bathsheba Taylor you shall be," Marcus said.

****

The pastor's parlor had lace curtains in the wide front window, and little lamb figurines on a side table with a tiny shepherdess in attendance. Mary Rose declined a wedding at the altar, saying God understood their hearts were true. Emma and the pastor's wife stood at the back of the room as witnesses.

She trembled, fighting an urge to run. *Patrick. I am standing here with Patrick.*

"Do you take this man…?" the pastor intoned, and his words droned on as a background buzzing to her fantasy. Her beloved stood at her shoulder and when instructed forced a thin silver band on her finger. Nothing valuable, for Patrick was a farmer, though these days he had taken up pig farming. She gazed up into his eyes, now a somber yellow-brown instead of a laughing green.

Their child must be named Patrick; and if a girl, Patricia. A small smile touched her lips as she responded. "I do."

Chapter Eighteen
Emma

Emma slung a saddle over Honor's tall ebony back. His long tail swished, but he held steady as she cinched the billet straps around his belly. After a brief ride, she would bathe, for this might be her last warm bath for months. She was expected to dine this evening with the newlyweds in the main house. Tomorrow at sunrise she would leave Wylder and head West.

The lonely trail ahead held great appeal after the chaotic weeks with her argumentative companions. Such peculiar fates claimed Clara and Mary Rose, who turned out to be far different from the innocent travelers she first supposed them to be. Were the private lives of most womenfolk so fraught and complicated? From her experience, women's days appeared calm and tedious, made up of housework, gossip and children. None of that appealed to Emma.

Horses, books, being outdoors—those were the essentials that made life worth living. She desired a quiet, peaceful future. One devoid of murder and betrayal.

She urged Honor into a trot as they approached the main road past the farm. His smooth muscles worked under her legs, and with a slight squeeze of her knees, he fell into an easy canter. Warm air brushed against her face and tugged at her hair. Open land with no sign of barbed wire or habitation all around. They left the road for the rougher terrain. Mature burr oak trees, their massive trunks and wide-spreading branches, dotted a field and minions of scrubby boxelder maples and their taller, more elegant cousins, the Rocky Mountain maples, clustered in groups of two and three. Underfoot were a riot of wildflowers in a rainbow of colors; pink yarrow and giant hyssop, white chamomile and golden arnica, along with a smattering of tiny button-sized blooms she didn't recognize.

They slowed to a walk, and Emma steered Honor away from a cluster of prickly thistles. His warm flanks exuded the steamy horse smell she loved, a unique scent that evoked home and comfort and all she had lost. Absent-mindedly, she tugged out the black scrap of lace from her pocket, a reminder she could never return. Home didn't exist anymore. She fingered the lace, caught between past, present and future. If Wyoming weren't so soured by Clara's arrest and Mary Rose's scheming, she might have considered staying in Wylder until next spring. The majesty of the mountains and unpeopled land had great appeal. Just as well she left tomorrow and stuck to her plan. If the law caught up with Clara, it might find her as well.

****

The October night she had fled from West Virginia was moonless. Dark clouds rolled in late that afternoon, two days before her trial, and provided the best and perhaps last opportunity to run. The only dark clothing she owned, and able to bear against her skin, was her grandmother's mourning gown, now sour from weeks of constant wear. How many deaths had this dress seen? It seemed appropriate to don this cheerless apparel for a final bereavement—the loss of her home and perhaps self-respect. Tonight, she intended to commit her first and only premeditated crime. Horse theft.

The Parker family sent no condolences over her father's death, though he worked for them his entire life. They had used him and thrown him away, and now planned to bury her as well. No one asked for her version of events, an account that laid at least partial blame on their dead son for the disastrous fire. She didn't need to be told the insurance company was more likely to pay in full if arson was the cause, rather than their son's lechery.

The damp autumn grass lay soft under her boots as she headed to the Parker farm. Gray trailed behind her on a lead, saddlebags loaded with food, clothing and—at the last minute—her father's pistol. The mule's ears stood erect and his eyes wide and alert at this unusual nighttime outing. His sure footing gave Emma courage. Shadowy shapes flitted above in the trees and the occasional glow of a firefly lit the darkness.

The empty spot where the long row of stables used to be came as a shock. The ground scarred by fire, black and accusing. The heavy scent of smoke and ash hung in the air despite its being weeks after the fire. Emma swallowed hard, her courage withered. A young man died here, taking with him the dreams and hopes of his family. She tugged at Gray's lead with the intent to return home and await the court's judgment. A soft nicker drew her attention to the old set of stables, which had escaped the inferno likely because of their separation by a small training ring.

"Wait here," she ordered Gray and dropped the lead. She didn't need to alarm the horses into a commotion with the presence of an unfamiliar animal. Her stomach clenched with the dread of which horses she wouldn't find in the stable, meaning they had perished in the fire or were destroyed. Tears prickled her eyes almost immediately. Where was Raven Head, Will-O-Wisp and Straight Shot? She glanced among the dozen horses in the stable and counted more than a dozen others she loved that weren't to be found.

Hurry. An inner warning told her she had little time to spare. Honor, a regal black, stared at her with solemn regard. One of the most valuable studs the Parkers owned. Fury replaced sorrow. She would take Honor. Her father's life was worth much more. In moments, she saddled the prized Thoroughbred and led him from the stall. A louder, more urgent nicker sounded from the next stall and she whirled, afraid of a disturbance. A young bay she hadn't seen before tossed its head and let forth a high-pitched whinny. Other horses shifted in their stalls and one stamped its hooves.

"Shush, all is well," she said softly. She glanced toward the mansion and a small structure, newly built, that must house the groundskeeper. No lights appeared. The horses settled—all but the bay, whose neck stretched over the stall door, with ears tilted forward. A beautiful narrow head, tall in the withers, bright eyes. Despite her hurry, Emma couldn't help but pause to admire this latest acquisition of the Parkers', clearly the start of a new line for their racing stables. A second Thoroughbred, along with Gray, was likely to mark her more easily in her flight. West Virginians knew their horse breeds, with many able to detail at a glance the lineage of the two horses she stole, even back to this very stable.

The bay kicked the side of her stall, a sharp crack like a gunshot, and the murmur of voices carried to Emma on the night air. She grabbed a bridle and slipped it over the animal's head. "Escape with us then, if you insist," she said in a low tone.

Quickly, she led the horses to Gray, tied the hem of her dark skirts between her legs, and with a slight hop to the high stirrup, mounted the black. As a final touch of concealment, she draped her grandmother's mourning veil over her head and tied it under her chin. She guided the animals at a trot toward a forest trail behind the old stables and into the darkness.

Within days, Emma regretted her impulse to snatch the troublesome bay. The young horse, a yearling at most, was skittish, stubborn and had a tendency to nip. Her burns broke open repeatedly, and the saddle scraped her skin raw. More than a dozen times during the first week her will broke, and she wished for capture if only to end the pain. If she were assured of being hanged, one quick snap of the neck to end it all, she might have given in. But the gentler sex was believed to be more pliable and able to be reformed to their natural moral nature. A dread of being locked up propelled her forward.

Days and weeks passed without a sign of a chase. Was the law so inept they were unable to hunt down a wounded girl and three large animals? In early December, after tracking south to avoid the bitter cold, she took a job mucking stalls in Louisiana in trade for food and shelter for herself and her three animal companions. An occasional tip came her way, and those purchased small extras—two pairs of trousers, two shirts and underclothes. She ripped a swatch off of the lacy veil and tucked it in her pocket; her only legacy. In late February, physically stronger and with the burns healed into pink and white puckered scars, she left Louisiana with a small pocket full of coin and a plan. There was a horse trader in Oregon.

****

Mary Rose greeted her at the door to the big house. A smile lit her face as though she hadn't seen Emma every day for weeks. "Come in. Dinner is nearly ready." She gestured toward the chairs near the fireplace. "Have a seat in our parlor while I finish in the kitchen."

A scrape and thump from above drew Emma's gaze to the ceiling.

Mary Rose smirked. "My husband is moving the armoire to another wall in the bedroom. He tries so hard to please me." She bustled away to the kitchen where steam escaped the lid of a pot on the stove.

Emma trailed behind her and leaned against the wall, taking in the aroma of savory ham and beans. On a shelf sat a silver service where canned goods had been stacked the day before. "I can carry bowls to the table," she offered.

"You are our guest and tomorrow you leave. Enjoy another page or two of that book over there while you wait for Pat—, er, my husband to come down." Mary Rose stirred furiously at the pot's contents.

Pity rose up in Emma, though Mary Rose didn't deserve it. Whatever make-believe game she played was unlikely to last a lifetime. In the room now dubbed the "parlor", Emma thumbed through a book but couldn't concentrate on the words. In the morning, she'd travel into the wilderness once more. A few more weeks and this long journey would be over. If she survived, though she was far more confident than when she first started out.

Heavy boots sounded on the stairs. "All done," Marcus called out. "As you requested."

Mary Rose met him at the bottom of the stairs. She tilted her face up to allow him to kiss her cheek. "You are a darling man."

His ears grew pink, and he gripped her around the waist to draw her nearer. Emma averted her gaze. Low murmurs and giggles reached her ears.

"A toast, to my new wife," Marcus called out.

Emma joined them at the table where Mary Rose poured wine into three glasses. They lifted their glasses and clinked them together before sipping.

"Now sit," Mary Rose ordered, "and I will serve."

Quiet descended while they ate. When Mary Rose refilled their bowls, Marcus addressed Emma. "I've set aside a few rashers of bacon and salt pork for your journey. And a knife, the best for butchering animals— or defending yourself, if it comes to that."

"Thank you." She squinted at him, recalling their conversation in the field the day she warned him about Mary Rose. People were complicated creatures and not to be trusted.

The wedding had been a fraud, she knew now. One more secret to add to those she already carried. Was it a crime to witness bigamy in action and not speak up?

She had kept her promise to Clara to warn him about Mary Rose. Full of good intentions, she had approached him in the field, aware the other woman observed them from the laundry line. Marcus stood stiffly as she imparted Clara's story about murder. "I

213

Julie Howard

believe she's dangerous," Emma had told him. "At the very least, she has no moral compass."

"Clara said something similar." He gazed out over the fields, lips thinned. "Mary Rose is a woman and won't get the best of me. I've learned my lesson."

Emma tried again. "There's a chance...there's every likelihood, as Clara swears...she killed her last husband. Why else did Mary Rose leave everything behind in Kansas? If she killed once, she might do it again." Her stomach tensed as she waited for his anger to erupt. She had made a serious accusation with no proof.

Instead of outrage, his voice grew tender. "I have a wife. She taught me the wicked nature of women."

Emma had gaped at him, horrified. "You have a wife? You're married?"

"She left me for a gambler, a slick-talking, no-good rascal. I didn't keep a close enough eye on her." His stare hardened. "She is likely dead, but even if she isn't, I doubt Hetty has the courage to face me again. Mary Rose need not worry."

"Surely you must tell her you may have a living wife?"

He shook his head. "You won't either. That woman needs a husband and I...I desire her greatly. Am I supposed to live alone forever? God has delivered her here for a reason. Do not interfere."

Emma hadn't intervened. The newly married couple at the table in front of her deserved a chance at a fresh start. None of them was innocent. Who was she to judge, after all? Crimes, large and small, swirled in the background while Mary Rose served a cherry cobbler. They didn't speak of Clara, who faced punishment for an offense she may not have committed.

"Thank you for your hospitality," Emma said again at the meal's end. "I'm very grateful." Mary Rose refused an offer of help with the dishes, cheeks flushed, every inch of her exuding joy in her outcome. Perhaps Marcus was right to seize happiness where possible—to consider the future instead of the past. She accepted a large package of victuals with thanks.

Mary Rose stopped her at the door. "Wait," she said. "I have a gift for you. Something for your new beginning." She ran upstairs, leaving Marcus and Emma alone for a moment.

"Take care of those extraordinary horses," he said. "I am sure they're worth a pretty penny."

She glanced at him sharply, but he said no more on the topic. Instead, he withdrew an envelope from his pocket. He stared at it for a moment and then thrust it to her. "From Clara. Read it later." He glanced over his shoulder at the sound of footsteps at the top of the stairs. "Put it in your pocket. I will not upset my wife on this happy day."

Emma tucked the letter away, grateful Marcus shared what news he had received.

Mary Rose hurried down the stairs with an armful of something wrapped in tissue. She handed it to Emma. "My yellow dress that I was married in. I will never marry again and so I want you to have it, though alterations will be necessary. Something to remember me by."

A dress was the last thing she needed, but Emma understood the message: Mary Rose promised to stay true to this husband. "Thank you. I doubt I'll ever forget you or this summer."

"Better than fiction?" Mary Rose said with a smile and linked one of her arms with Marcus'.

Brilliant crimson and purple filled the horizon as the sun continued on its own adventure around the world. Emma crossed the gap between the houses, her arms laden with gifts. Her scant belongings already bundled and heaped on the floor, she dropped the tissue-wrapped package on the table and opened Clara's letter. Beautiful script covered one page.

Dearest Marcus,

You must not be angry at me any longer. I have confessed and can only hope God will forgive me.

This judge has no taste for hanging women, especially since I've admitted my guilt and displayed a desire for penitence. I am to be sent to a reformatory and assigned duties befitting my gender and to learn from labor, discipline, and religious contemplation. In time, I may be released into the custody of a respectable household where, under the guidance of good people, I can assist with laundry, cooking and sewing during the day.

I fall frequently into meditation about the role of women in this perfect Creation. The Bible speaks of our sinful nature and the need for men's governance. My soul rebels against this truth, perhaps a sign of my feeble understanding. I hear talk, however, of a rising up of women who protest a "primitive" Bible compiled by priests, and who believe women are men's equals in every way in God's eyes. My dear brother, I am a sinner and I shall seek to quell such muddled thoughts.

Today, the sun hangs glorious in the sky. Strange, how the little fact of a bright sky soothes my heart. This same sun shines down on you. I wish you well.

You loving sister, Clara

P.S. Please do not wed Mary Rose. She is more like me than I realized, with a soul that rebels against men's dominance. The difference between us, however, is she is unrepentant and thus will be a troublesome wife.

Emma folded the letter and left it on the table for Marcus. Or Mary Rose, who would bristle at being likened to Clara in any way.

****

Emma rose before dawn, wishing to take advantage of the long summer days to travel. Already, though early August, night arrived sooner. The horses carried light packs to spare these prized assets undue burden. Gray's packs bulged with supplies; the mule's dark eyes alive and head up, he appeared to understand a new adventure loomed. Marcus appeared on his doorstep to wave goodbye. There was no sign of Mary Rose.

Emma nudged Honor forward, with Faith and Gray following behind. A high whinny sounded from the barn; Clara's mare, Lucky, called out a long, mournful farewell.

Chapter Nineteen
Emma, four years later

Nate Collins' arm muscles flexed as he pounded fence posts in place. Nate, twenty-eight with sun-kissed auburn hair and brown eyes flecked with green, a solid block of a man with an easy way around horses and had showed up one day at Emma's seaside ranch, seeking work. Two years later, she relied on him completely. He did the labor of three men without complaint and, like few others, paid her respect not as a woman but as his boss.

Emma reined in Nautilus, the eight-year-old chestnut gelding she acquired for the ranch and renamed for the ship in *Twenty Thousand Leagues Under the Sea*. She tried not to stare at Nate's bare chest. Must he strip half-naked to do his work? There was no way she would demand he don his shirt, and thus betray herself distracted by his well-formed, honey-tanned torso.

He halted his work and gave her a nod in greeting. "Several of these new posts are rotten. Murray owes you at least half a dozen in replacement. I can head to his place later and deal with this, if you'd like."

"I need you here. Send Jonathan," she said with a gesture at a dark-haired wiry man piling stones on a cart. "The field clearing can wait—the fence can't." In another paddock, Honor grazed, the pride of the farm, with stud fees every bit as high as she'd hoped. The horse trader near Portland continued to send a steady stream of business her way. Earlier this year, one of Honor's progeny showed well at a prominent southern California racetrack.

Nate laid a hand on the post he had just set into the ground. "It'll be done by week's end. You're certain cattle is the way to go?"

His unspoken words lingered between them: *For a woman.* Cattle was rugged work. She had sought his opinion months ago and though he cautioned her against it, a sideline in beef could pay for the additional acreage she desired. "There's profit in cattle. You should be glad of it; money pays your wages."

With that, she nudged her horse forward. She hadn't meant to be sharp with her words, but a pulse throbbing at the base of his smooth throat made her edgy. No hammer sounded against another post, and she knew he watched her ride away, his gaze boring into her back. She urged Nautilus into a canter. She had something more important to do than ogle her hired hand's bare chest.

A wind whipped up and carried with it a taste of the ocean. By the time she finished her errand to her nearest neighbor's house, three miles away, salt would lay like grit on her cheeks and forehead. In her pocket was two dollars, a price she had agreed upon three months earlier. Foolish, to spend money in this manner with so much work yet to be done on the ranch. But she'd promised herself. And besides, she deserved this treat.

****

The trek to the Pacific Ocean four years earlier

219

nearly broke her. The mountain ranges west of the Wyoming Territory proved difficult to traverse and the river crossings had been treacherous. Though it was still late August, a blizzard snowed her in for two nights. A week later, along a scenic creek, she ate a handful of tart red berries and fell so ill from vomiting and diarrhea she thought she might die. The usual cuts and bruises, blisters, and body aches from long days in the saddle became routine. When she arrived at the broad Columbia River, the going was easier. She tasted the river water each day and as it grew saltier and the river wider, winds whipping up whitecaps on its surface, she understood the great ocean neared.

Emma kissed Faith goodbye on her nose and fought back tears when at long last they met the trader. "Have a good life, my friend. Run hard. Never give up."

Honor nickered as the trader led the young bay to her destiny. Emma counted the cash, a huge amount along with a promise from the trader to send customers her way to mate their mares with Honor.

Unlike many places, Oregon had long allowed unmarried women to own property. Faith's sale enabled her to purchase thirty cleared acres with an option for thirty more of raw land if she completed the deal within five years. A well-built large barn, with an adjacent sheepherder's quarters, was the only structure on the land.

The trader kept his word and Honor generated enough in stud fees the first two years to purchase a nine-year-old draft horse, five goats, materials for a paddock fence, and the hiring of two men to build the fence and clear the fields for planting. The men shared a small bunkhouse on the far side of the property, and she lived in the one-room sheepherder's hut, a treat compared to a bedroll on the ground. The greatest luxury was knowing the four walls, barn, and land belonged to her.

Nate sauntered into the barn one day while she was pinning up her hair. "I hear you could use an extra man."

In the doorway, silhouetted by the sun behind him, she squinted to see him properly. "Who sent you?"

"Silas Anderson, down the road, says he knows you."

Emma nodded; if Silas sent this man to her, it meant a great deal. Silas and his wife, Mary, owned five hundred acres and one of the best run ranches in the region. Mary stopped by once a month with gossip and any mail she might have gathered from Skipanon, the nearest town with a post office. The mail always included a packet of newspapers from Wylder, Wyoming.

"I can use another hand, one who works hard." She set the last pin securely in her hair, annoyed he caught her in such an intimate act. "Willing to do any job, however small."

They agreed on terms quickly. Nate stated firmly that he required two days a week off but promised to work dawn to dusk the other days. Any other man she'd have sent packing for such an arrogant demand. But then he grinned, and his whole face lit up—hazel eyes twinkling, creases at the sides of his mouth indicating a cheerful temperament—and she smiled back and agreed.

Only then had he nodded toward her modest

housing in the corner of the barn and made this offer: "Silas says you need a proper house. I have an aptitude for carpentry." He raised his eyebrows in question.

This afternoon, as she brushed Honor's coat to ready him to service two mares the next morning, she recalled the smile that had brightened Nate's face, as though she'd given him the world and not just a job. She patted Honor's sleek neck. "You have become quite the ladies' man, my friend. Let's give the girls their money's worth."

Two black and white pups whimpered in a straw-lined crate, which lay on the floor of the barn while she worked. Next to the crate lay two unopened letters and a newspaper Mary Anderson had given her along with the pups. Emma didn't dare turn the young dogs loose among the livestock, for fear they would be crushed underfoot. Their parents were superior cattle dogs; she'd been eyeing them since she first met Silas and Mary, whose dogs were known throughout the county for their herding instincts. A dollar a piece for pick of the litter they said.

Nate strode into the barn, heavy boots crunching straw and gravel. He chuckled at the sight of the dogs. "Who do we have here?" He kneeled beside the crate and the pups yipped and wriggled with pleasure at his attention.

"It's my birthday present to myself," she said, the words escaping her mouth. The sight of his large body crouched over the crate melted her heart.

He glanced up. "Your birthday? We must celebrate."

She shrugged and continued brushing Honor's coat. "Not worth a celebration. Twenty-three years on this earth is nothing special to observe. I promised myself cattle dogs. They're plenty."

"Allow me to celebrate it for you then. I shall ride to town this moment and dance until dawn."

She laughed at the idea. Nate's large frame didn't appear made for dancing, though he carried himself easily enough on the ranch. Inside, he had to duck ever-so-slightly to clear doorways and his bulk filled a room. Outside, though, he was a graceful creature, his actions about the ranch fluid and straightforward. His broad shoulders swung saddles atop the horses with ease and he never seemed to tire.

He joined in her laughter, enjoying the joke on himself, and appeared pleased with himself. He rose and propped one elbow against the stall, those thick arms heavy with muscle. A good man. A twinge of longing and regret hit her anew.

"Emma?" His voice broke into her musing, his gaze tender as though he read her mind.

Damnation. He was her hired hand and a fine one at that. She must not moon over something that could never happen. Nate Collins should find a sweet girl in Astoria with smooth, soft skin and a gentle nature. A woman who wore a dress, at least.

"Steiner's bringing two mares in the morning. Make sure he pays the full fee upfront this time." She slapped down the brush. "Finish up with Honor, will you?"

She gripped the crate with the puppies and stomped to the house, annoyed with him for stirring up feelings within her. Nearly five years after the fire, her skin had toughened into permanent scars. The incident marked her, ruined her. Even in the unlikely event a man looked past the scars, questions were likely to follow, ones she couldn't answer truthfully. Men had died at her hand. The ghosts of Gilbert and the two horse thieves still haunted her dreams.

Loosened from their confinement, the puppies ran and tumbled in the narrow two-story farmhouse Nate had built the previous year. Masonry at the bottom to keep moisture at bay, and then tall wood studs stretched to the roofline. One bedroom, a kitchen and sitting room on the first floor, complete with a chamber-pot closet so she didn't need to visit the outhouse at night or during chilly winter months.

The entire second level consisted of one large room, and red maple flooring of wide, smooth planks. This was her reading room, with windows on three sides that flooded the space with light and provided splendid views of her property. Nate's talent showed in every exposed rafter beam, tightly-fitted wood joints, and the solid roof. The fragrance of new wood, redolent of a new life, hung on the air. A huge improvement over the cramped sheepherder's room in the barn.

A puddle appeared under one of the pups. Emma hurried to clean the mess and then scooped up the dog and headed to the door. They needed to learn the rules. As she approached the door, a knock startled her. She expected no one.

When she opened the door, Nate stood, hat in hand. "As it's your birthday, I thought I'd show you something."

"You are persistent."

"An advantageous quality."

She set the pup down and scooted it outside, away from the threshold. "Depends on the situation, I think."

"Come, Emma. I have something to celebrate as well." An element of pleading entered his expression and tone. "There's no one I'd rather share this with."

The words jolted her. They had progressed beyond employer and employee; at some point, they'd become friends. Nothing more. "What do you want to show me?"

He gestured toward the edge of her land. "Over there. Let's take the horses."

Nothing stirred in the direction he pointed, but he had captured her full attention. If something had occurred on or near her property, she needed to know. "What took you over there? As far as I know, there's nothing except poison ivy and a dry creek bed. Not even a road."

A secret smile crossed his face, which infuriated her and roused her curiosity even more. She set the puppy in its crate—perhaps she'd solicit Nate's opinion on names for them—and went with him to the barn to saddle the horses.

****

Emma dismounted and stared. Fence stakes lined an area, ostensibly for a corral. Stones already had been cleared from one area and stacked up into a rock wall along the far side. Lumber lay on the ground, ready to be utilized in a building project. Dismay swept through her. How had she not noticed or heard about a new owner in the area? Silas hadn't whispered a word. This adjoining parcel of land would have been nice to purchase someday in the future. She twisted to Nate, who stood next to her. "Who is the owner?"

He beamed. "Yer looking at him."

"You!" She gaped at him before returning her gaze

to the land and tried not to let her dismay show. "How long since you purchased it? How did you afford all this on the salary I pay you?"

"Silas filed the option on the land for me when I first arrived at your place to work," he explained. "I paid him back bit by bit, and also I had a little savings. He's a cousin on my mother's side, you know."

"I didn't know. He never told me." Emma chaffed at the secret kept by a neighboring landowner and her employee. "Neither did you."

"I wanted this to be a surprise, though I expected you to ride out this way sooner but you never did."

"I did not expect a neighbor to materialize so suddenly." A pit opened up in her stomach as she recognized what this meant. Nate's familiar form on her ranch, his friendly chatter and cheerful demeanor would be gone, focused on improving his own land.

His smile disappeared. "You might congratulate me."

Feeling churlish, Emma put a foot in the stirrup and threw her other leg over her mount. "Yes. You've done well for yourself. I suppose you'll give notice now you have this land."

"I didn't plan to leave your employ so soon. Not until next spring, at least."

Tears sprang and spilled before she was able to avert her face. She brushed them away and forced herself to behave better for his sake. "Don't mind me. I am happy for you, Nate. You deserve to do better than working on someone else's ranch. And we will be neighbors."

He climbed into the saddle, his countenance troubled. "I hope we remain friends. And perhaps—"

Emma kicked Nautilus forward, before more hurtful words landed on her ears. She drove her horse into a gallop, leaving Nate far behind. Her burn scars were a barbed wire fence around her body and soul; no one allowed in—or out.

Twenty minutes later, a pounding rattled her door. Nate, red-faced and chest heaving, filled the doorway. He heaved a sigh. "Why do you make me chase you all over the countryside today?"

She backed from the door and allowed him in. The puppies raced forward and chewed at his boot laces. "Forgive me. I'm ill-tempered today and gave you the brunt of it. Please have coffee with me. And tell me your plans for your land."

He scooped up both puppies in one hand and lifted them to his face. They licked every inch of his chin and neck, their round bodies wriggling in joy. "I'd enjoy a cup. Have you named these critters yet?"

Emma lit the stove to reheat the morning coffee, enough left for two more cups. She glanced over her shoulder to where Nate now crouched playing with the dogs. "Any suggestions?"

He gave the pups an assessing gaze. Their black bodies with white and tan markings were almost identical; one, however, had an extra dab of white on his chest. This one now play-growled at his brother, who scampered across the room. "General," Nate decided. "He's a bossy one, who likes to give orders. Even has a medal on his chest for bravery."

Emma laughed and brought the coffee into the room. "And the other?"

"Puck, the clown from Shakespeare, you know. He keeps the general from getting too high and mighty."

As though to prove this point, Puck sped back across the room and leaped onto General. The two wrestled merrily.

Nate heaved his frame into a chair. They sipped their coffee in companionable silence and watched the dogs wage their mock battle. "I admire you a great deal, Emma, as you must know by now," he said as though they were in the middle of a conversation on the topic.

Her shoulders stiffened. She glanced up and her throat closed at the sight of the yearning in his expression. Her hand trembled as she set her cup on a side table.

"I didn't speak sooner because I had nothing to offer," he continued. "You've seen my land today; it'll provide a good living." He hesitated then soldiered on. "I suspect you have feelings for me too."

"Nate, I can't...I won't...this isn't possible." She refused to lie and say she didn't care for him. She rose from her chair, the little hairs on her arms tingling and heart hammering. Actually, every part of her felt awake—except scarred skin left numb by flames.

His voice was quiet and somber. "Give me one reason, tell me you don't feel the same way, and I'll never speak again."

Emma matched his tone. "You have no idea what fire does to skin."

He leaned back in his chair, assessing her as though he dared her to show him. Then let him be horrified. Let him run. Tears of anger and frustration welled up and threatened to spill out. Turning her back on him, she unbuttoned her blouse and yanked it out of her waistband. Behind her, she pictured his avid gaze prepared for a pleasing female form. She ripped off her blouse and unbuttoned her pants. There was no mistaking this disrobing for an act of love. She kept her back to him while she kicked off her trousers and stood in nothing but a light chemise and short drawers that stopped at mid-thigh.

Taking a deep breath, Emma called upon years of rage; the attempted rape, and the inferno that ensued and consumed so many lives, both human and horse. The loss of home and an ordinary body. Her ability to kill two horse thieves and walk away without regret. She was an aberration. Let Nate see.

She untied the drawstring at her waist and let the drawers fall to her ankles. Let him bear witness to the ripples of ugly pink scar tissue across her hip and down one leg. A nightmare of misshapen flesh. His sharp intake of breath pierced her heart. She fought down a sob. She would miss his presence around the ranch, their easy conversations, his joyful disposition.

A touch stilled her breath.

His lips traced the scars and his large, capable hands light on her hips. Anguish so long imprisoned broke free. Tears streamed down her cheeks. Gentle kisses traced up her back and round one shoulder. "Emma," he whispered as he unbraided her hair. "My Emma. The strongest woman I've ever met."

She leaned back into his powerful chest and inhaled his musky male scent, mixed with labors of the day. His hands stretched around her and unbuttoned her chemise. She stepped out of her drawers and turned to face him. Tears dampened his cheeks, and sorrow and desire filled his eyes.

"You are a woman to be reckoned with."

"I suppose." Her voice shook, her emotions

unfettered and raw. A new feeling surged inside, one that made her dizzy and clearheaded at the same time.

In seconds, he shrugged off his shirt, the rest of his clothes, and they were in her bedroom before she fathomed how they got there. Her body, so long a burden, now sang with pleasure. Who knew?

After, he cradled her in his arms.

"Do you think there's natural justice in the world?" she asked, staring at a corner of the ceiling where a long-legged spider had taken up residence.

Nate propped himself up on one elbow and faced her. "You mean fairness?" He shook his head firmly. "No. Otherwise, there'd be a whole lot of angry rabbits complaining about being low on the food chain."

A smile touched her lips. "Amongst people, then."

"Too many unscrupulous people end up rewarded, it seems, for any fairness. I believe in a broad justice at work, as though the world plays a balancing act. Five good actions here balance five dishonest actions in, say, Boston."

She stared at the ceiling and considered this possibility. "It doesn't seem right that someone else would pay for my crimes."

"I can't imagine you doing anything wrong. Certainly not crimes."

Her stomach twisted. The intimacy they just shared contrasted with unspoken lies. He needed to know her past or none of this was real. "I killed two men who tried to steal my horses. They weren't even my horses; I stole them."

Nate traced the scars on her hip. His fingers trailed down her leg to where the burn marks ended. Two deep frown lines furrowed his forehead. Birdsong filtered through the window. The house creaked in the silence. This is how it ends, she thought, before anything really began. But the secret carried too much weight for her to bear alone. Let the consequences fall where they may.

"There's more." The words sounded loud after the long quiet. "I may be—partially—to blame for another man's death." She dropped her voice to a whisper. "And a fire."

His hand rested on her hip. One puppy, on a cushion against one wall, whimpered and shifted in his sleep. "Is that everything?"

She nodded and trembled. Hope and desire, dangling by a thread, hurt worse than a thousand fires.

His chest rose and fell with a big breath. "I felt your sadness when we first met. I wondered what happened in your past, and who hurt you."

"Me?"

"It makes me want to protect you and keep you from any more hurt."

"Pity," she said.

"Not pity," he said firmly. "I admire you. I suspect you had some pretty good reasons for your actions. Maybe someday you'll tell me about it."

Emma closed her eyes. If he was willing to hear more, he planned to stay. "You're a good man, Nate Collins."

Firm lips warm against hers and his arms drew her close. "Right now, I'm done talking."

****

Much later, when they had lit candles to chase the dark away, she told him about Gilbert and the fire. About her father, stealing Honor and Faith, and how she killed the two horse thieves for a similar crime.

231

About Clara, Mary Rose, Marcus, and Hetty. Her trek through the treacherous Lolo Pass in Idaho Territory. The candles burned low, flickered out, and still she talked until there were no secrets left unsaid. Even her middle name—Constance—which was not a secret, but a part of herself she wanted him to know.

He held her tight, and she felt the scars on her heart shrivel and shrink and disappear. The night softened into a pinkish-gray and a touch of gold filtered through the window. Trills and chirps welcomed the sun, and with a glance at the man who slumbered on her pillow, Emma realized there might not be justice but if she tried, there could be happiness.

Chapter Twenty
Emma, Mary Rose and Clara

Later, weary and satisfied from a full day of chores, puppies at her feet, Emma opened the first of two letters Mary Anderson handed her the day before when she purchased the dogs. Familiar handwriting covered the page along with ink blots from a careless hand unused to wielding a pen.

Out the window, Nate pounded posts into the ground to finish her new corral. He'd work until the last glimmer of light left the sky. Only then would he knock on her door. She tore her gaze away and read:

Dearest Friend,

I apologize for the long delay in writing. My life is very full with little time to sit and write.

Our Patrick counts to ten now, a little genius. Ten toes, ten ears of corn, ten piglets. He will make a fine banker someday. Joseph and Lila, our one-year-old twins, started walking all at once the same day and are determined to climb every surface and break their heads open. I am both besotted and nearly deranged by the demands of motherhood, with yet another due this winter. Children have ruined my figure, but Marcus says he loves his plump little wife. As for me, what a relief to dispense with a corset; I wear one to church and town, of course, but there's no need on the farm.

I'm happy to hear your ranch is a success. At my

urging, my husband will give up the nasty hog business after this next batch is sold and plant the farm in wheat. He heeds my advice and has even bought another milk cow. I make butter and sell it to pay for household needs. Marcus says I'm very clever.

Clara sent another letter last month, her first in a year. Her letters are quite tedious and say nothing interesting. She makes quilts for the children's home and assists in the Reformatory kitchen. Not a word about the other inmates who must have committed fascinating crimes.

Who would have expected, Emma, that you and I would become pen pals? We are the same in many ways, though, aren't we? Strong-spirited survivors. We would never have confessed our crimes, had we any, and gone meek as a mouse to jail.

Send me more ideas for books to read. I did not care for your suggestion of Frankenstein. *The story scared me nearly out of my wits and I do not believe a woman wrote that book. I cheered aloud when the monster died. Recommend a story that speaks of first loves and their enduring nature.*

We have a boarder, a woman named Hetty who lives in the small house. She appeared one day dressed nearly in rags. She must be about forty years old but looks to be sixty. Life has been hard for her, I believe. I'm not surprised at Marcus' generosity in aiding this stranger—he took you and me in, didn't he? She helps with the children and laundry but doesn't seem to be fond of me. Perhaps, like you, she will become my friend in time.

Oh, the twins are screaming about something, and Hetty is in the barn with Marcus. Must I do everything myself? Do write soon.

Bathsheba (Mary Rose) Taylor

Emma set the letter to one side, contemplating the reappearance of Hetty in Wylder. Poor Mary Rose! Poor Hetty, too! How long until Marcus's first wife insisted on her proper and legal role? And Mary Rose with children. Would they all live together in quasi-marital disharmony? She shook her head at the strange turn of events. If she knew anything, however, Mary Rose wouldn't go down without a fight.

Puck chewed at her sock, his sharp puppy teeth nipping through the fabric. Emma scooped him up and kissed a roll of fat on his neck. She inhaled his sweet breath and set him on her lap. "You little rascal. Behave yourself." The dog curled up and fell sleep.

The second letter filled her with apprehension. Clara wrote every couple of months, ever since Emma initiated correspondence three years earlier. Although their time together had been brief, the intense events of the summer she traveled with the two women lingered in her mind. They hadn't been friends, but a lasting bond had been forged through extraordinary events. Clara's imprisonment unsettled her, the injustice of it.

Dear Emma,

Thank you for your last letter and the three silver dollars inside. What a delightful and unexpected surprise! You must be careful about sending money, however. My mail can be opened by guards at any time and I'm sorry to say one or two are not honest sorts. In any case, you should not send money at all as the state of Missouri provides for all my needs.

I hope you are well and the animals you love too. You will have to write and let me know if you were able to get a puppy from your neighbors.

Emma smiled and scratched Puck's round belly. One of the puppy's hind legs made slow circles in appreciation of the tummy rub.

It has been a most unusual few months. I don't know who to tell other than you. I write to my brother but only Mary Rose writes back. (I will not refer to her as Bathsheba as that name is ridiculous.) You know my reasons for not trusting her with anything other than the most bland news.

I have a secret, which is a miracle within these walls with no privacy. Over the past year, I have developed a friendship with one of the guards. He is a kind man, courteous to all the women, and never treats any of us as criminals. Frederick is a widower with five grown children and eight grandchildren, though only fifty-seven years old. We have taken to meeting in the laundry where I sometimes work, and also in the garden during my free hour. I've learned he has made his own mistakes—he tells me these things in confidence as we have built a trust between us. More than a trust; he says he loves me and will wait for me, as long as it takes. As you can imagine, our relationship is prohibited so we must be circumspect.

Yes! I kept this secret even from you because, before now, there seemed no future with Frederick. Yesterday, his eldest son, John, visited me. John is a lawyer with three children of his own and knows my story. He says he will file an appeal, claiming I confessed under duress.

My behavior while here should speak in my favor. At the very least, he expects these efforts to reduce my sentence, and he believes I may even receive a parole before too many more years go by.

Now I'm afraid you must indulge me a few lines of complaint. John says women often are denied justice. He has met Mrs. Elizabeth Cady Stanton and found her formidable! He says women's suffrage will happen, but not without a great struggle. Oh, why are women pitted against men in this world when we have been put on Earth together as companions?

Frederick supports my beliefs about the equality of women and does not see them as counter to God and church. I used to believe I was sinful for my way of thinking, but now I realize I was right all along.

Emma, I am very fortunate to love and be loved. I wish the same for you someday.

Kitchen duty beckons and I must go. I will give this letter to Frederick to mail as I wouldn't want another guard to open and read all I have disclosed.

Faithfully,

Clara

Emma rubbed her eyes in the fading light and set the puppy on the floor to join his brother. The pounding of posts had ceased and a thrill went through her at the thought of Nate and all that was ahead for them. Somehow, she, Mary Rose and Clara had survived the worst months of their lives and seized a new beginning.

A rap sounded at the door and her heart skipped in happiness. She hurried to open the door and Nate stood there, chest heaving as though he had run a mile.

She would write to her friends later. Much later.

A word about the author...

Julie Howard is the author of the Wild Crime and Spirited Quest series. She is a former journalist and editor who has covered topics ranging from crime to cowboy poetry and is a member of the Idaho Writers Guild.

Visit her at: http://www.juliemhoward.com

Thank you for purchasing
this publication of The Wild Rose Press, Inc.

For questions or more information
contact us at
info@thewildrosepress.com.

The Wild Rose Press, Inc.
www.thewildrosepress.com